"Why don't we have boyfriends?"

"Pam, we don't even have dates," I said. "How do you expect us to have *boyfriends*?"

"I don't know. Can't you just buy them at the supermarket?"

"Wouldn't that be nice? Hello, Mr. Groceryman. What aisle do you keep the boyfriends in?"

"Do you carry the tall, dark, handsome brand?" Pam added. "The kind with long eyelashes?" We laughed.

If only it were that easy, I thought.

Other Bullseye Books you will enjoy

And the Other, Gold by Susan Wojciechowski

Beanpole by Barbara Park

Marci's Secret Book of Flirting (Don't Go Out Without It!) by Jan Gelman

Patty Dillman of Hot Dog Fame by Susan Wojciechowski

The Sisters Impossible by James D. Landis

Marci's Secret Book of Dating

by Jan Gelman

BULLSEYE BOOKS

ALFRED A. KNOPF ♥ NEW YORK

A Bullseye Book Published by Alfred A. Knopf, Inc.
Copyright © 1991 by Jan Gelman
Cover art copyright © 1991 by Dan Burr

Library of Congress Cataloging-in-Publication Data
Gelman, Jan.
Marci's secret book of dating / Jan Gelman. p. cm.
Summary: Hoping to snare a date in time for the seventh-
grade Valentine's Day dance, Marci sets out to study and mas-
ter the fundamentals of dating and develops a crush on the
cute but inconsiderate Patrick.
ISBN 0-679-81106-0 (pbk.) ISBN 0-679-91106-5 (lib. bdg.)
[1. Dating (Social customs)—Fiction] I. Title.
PZ7.G2836Maq 1991 [Fic]—dc20 90-2255

RL: 4.7

First Bullseye Books edition: August 1991

Manufactured in the United States of America
10 9 8 7 6 5 4 3 2 1

To my mother, whose passion for travel and fascination with different cultures inspired me to pack my bags and seek out foreign lands

And to my Balinese mentor, Ratu Aji Sangka, and all the other incredible people I met during my year's journey around the world

"Look who's heading our way," said my best friend, Pam, as we sat in the open-air lunch area at Franklin Junior High School. It was Leslie Weber, walking arm in arm with her boyfriend, Peter Johnson. *The* Peter Johnson. Mister Popularity.

Leslie made sure to walk Peter by our lunch table. "Hi, girls," she said smugly. Peter smiled and waved at us as they passed. We waved back. Then I rolled my eyes and looked meaningfully at Pam.

"It doesn't seem fair," Pam said when Leslie had gone by. "Why don't we have boyfriends?"

"Pam, we don't even have dates," I said. "How do you expect us to have *boyfriends*?"

"I don't know. Can't you just buy them at the supermarket?"

"Wouldn't that be nice? Hello, Mr. Groceryman. What aisle do you keep the boyfriends in?"

"Do you carry the tall, dark, handsome brand?" Pam added. "The kind with long eyelashes?" We laughed.

If only it were that easy, I thought. Ever since we

started seventh grade four months ago, Pam and I had been watching kids pair off. It seemed as if every girl in Franklin Junior High had a boyfriend. Everyone except us. I thought it was because I was too fat or my brown hair was ugly. But Pam told me I was crazy, that there wasn't a thing wrong with me. Besides, Pam was a knockout blond—and she didn't have a boyfriend either.

"What do the girls with boyfriends have that we don't?" asked Pam.

"I don't know. Leslie is a loud, obnoxious gossip queen. I don't want to be like her."

"Me neither. But maybe there's something they have that we're missing." Pam rested her chin on her hand and stared thoughtfully past me at all the couples who were sitting around on the lawn. It had rained in Los Angeles most of December, but the new year had kicked off with beautiful weather and everyone was enjoying the sunshine.

"Look at them," Pam said. I followed her eyes to one of the couples. The girl wasn't all *that* pretty. "Why does *she* have a boyfriend?"

"Good question," I said. "Let's make notes about each girl with a boyfriend. Then maybe we can figure out what they have in common and come up with a formula for getting dates."

"Great idea," said Pam. "This can be our dating book."

A few months ago Pam and I had decided we wanted to know how to flirt. We kept flirting notes in a book, and we really learned how to do it! I still had the book hidden under my mattress.

I pulled out my math notebook and opened it to an empty page. "Let's start with Leslie and Peter."

I wrote:

COUPLE MISSION
MONDAY

1. LESLIE AND PETER—LESLIE IS THIN AND HAS BROWN EYES AND CURLY BROWN HAIR THAT SHE FLIPS BACK A LOT WITH HER HANDS. SHE LOVES TO GOSSIP BUT SAYS SHE DOESN'T.

2. GRASS COUPLE—THE GIRL IS KIND OF FAT, HAS SHORT BROWN HAIR AND A NARROW FACE. SHE SMILES A LOT.

"Quick, look over there," Pam said, nudging me. "She's on student council and he's the ninth-grade treasurer."

I wrote:

3. STUDENT COUNCIL GIRL AND TREASURER—SHE IS TALL, PRETTY AND VERY TAN. WEARS FORM-FITTING CLOTHES AND LOOKS GREAT IN THEM. SHE'S PROBABLY SMART, TOO.

I looked around for more couples. I saw a girl from my science class at a table near us. She was sitting next to her boyfriend, who was pretty cute although he had a big nose. They were both in seventh grade.

I added to the list:

4. CAROLINE AND STEVE—CAROLINE IS SHORT WITH LIGHT-BROWN STRAIGHT HAIR. SHE'S SHY, A SCIENCE BRAIN AND VERY NICE.

For the remainder of lunch we analyzed each girl who passed us with a boy. Some were tall. Some were short. Some were pretty. Some weren't. There were girls with brown hair, red hair, blond hair, black hair. We saw a girl from the choir, and one from the tennis team, and one who worked in the library. Our search for a common trait—the something special that made them girlfriend material—seemed futile.

"So," Pam finally said, tilting her head to one side and squinting her eyes.

"So what?" I asked. Pam always tilted her head like that when she was concocting something.

"We need to find ourselves some boyfriends."

"So what else is new?" I sighed. "The question is, how?"

"I don't know. But Marci, what are we going to do if we don't have dates for the Valentine's Day dance?"

The Valentine's Day dance was one of the biggest events of the year, like the prom in high school. And it was less than six weeks away. Two years ago when my sister, Darlene, was in the eighth grade, she didn't have a date for the dance because she had just broken up with her boyfriend. She cried about it for weeks.

"Let's make a pact," said Pam.

"What kind of a pact?" I asked suspiciously. Somehow Pam always managed to get us into embarrassing situations.

"That we have to have boyfriends by Valentine's Day."

"What about just having to have dates?"

"Oh, come on," she said. "Dating's too easy. We need to aim higher. We can do it. We learned how to flirt, didn't we?"

"Well, yes," I said. "But that was different."

When we decided that we wanted to learn how to flirt, we asked Cathy, my old baby-sitter, for advice. She actually mailed us flirting instructions from college in Colorado. We practiced smiling, making eye contact and starting conversations. By now we were pros. We could *meet* almost any guys we wanted. But just because we met them didn't mean they were going to ask us out. I wish Cathy hadn't gone off to study in England this semester. We could sure use her help.

"Come on, Marci." Pam brushed her bangs out of her eyes with her hand. "You met Dave by flirting, didn't you?"

"Yes," I admitted.

Dave was kind of my boyfriend a few months ago. He was really nice, but we never had much to say to each other. He'd call and say, "Hi. How are you?" And then I'd say, "Great. How are you?" And then maybe we would talk about school. Or there would just be silence. Eventually he would say, "Well, I just called to say hi," or I would say, "Well, I better go," and we would hang up.

Somehow talking to boys on the phone was harder than talking to them in person. Besides, it was different talking to a boy than it was talking to a girl. Half the conversations Pam and I had were about boys. And you can't talk to boys about that! After a while Dave's phone calls stopped. We were still friends, but I didn't see him very often.

"Marci, we're almost thirteen! If we don't work on this now, we may be single forever. Now put up your right hand and repeat after me."

I shrugged and raised my hand.

"I, Marci Miller, will have a boyfriend by Valentine's Day," she said.

I repeated it.

Pam held her hand up. "And I, Pam Stevens, will have a boyfriend by Valentine's Day."

We shook on it.

My mom picked Pam and me up from school that day in our slightly battered station wagon. Timmy, my five-year-old brother, and Ninja, our new Scotty puppy, were in the car.

"Watch out for Ninja!" Timmy squealed as we climbed in. Ninja licked my face and then jumped on Pam.

"Hey, you little mutt!" Pam screeched. Ninja was tugging on her sweater. "Let go!"

You really had to keep your eyes on Ninja. He had already chewed the edges of our living room curtains into fringes, my straw beachbag was in shreds and I was missing several socks. "Thank God I'm home," Pam joked when we pulled up to her house. "I wouldn't have a sweater left if I stayed much longer."

"Bye, Pammy," Timmy said. He made barking noises. "Ninja says bye too."

"Bye, Timmy," she said. "Bye, Ninja. Thanks for the ride, Mrs. Miller." Then she turned to me and whispered, "Transfer our boyfriend notes into a new notebook."

"Aye, aye, Captain," I said, saluting.

When I got home, Darlene was lying on the couch in the living room. Ninja pounced on her.

"Get away from me!" she shouted, pushing him off the couch.

"Will one of you girls take Ninja for a walk?" my mother asked.

I was about to say yes when Darlene snapped, "I'm not taking him anywhere."

"It's your turn!" I said, my voice rising. Boy, her attitude really bugged me!

"What do you mean, it's my turn? I took him last time," Darlene said. She flipped her blond hair to one side with her hand. "Besides, I'm sick."

She always had an excuse. "You never do anything around here," I said. It was true. I always offered to help Mom cook, clean and watch Timmy. Darlene spent all of her time shopping, curling her hair and going out with her latest boyfriend, Bill.

"Girls, I don't think it's too much for me to ask that one of you takes *your* dog for a walk," my mother said.

"Fine, I'll do it," I said. I picked up Ninja's leash and clipped it to his collar.

"Thank you, Marci," my mom said.

I flashed Darlene my nastiest look. "Well, *somebody's* got to," I huffed, and walked out the door.

I never understood how Mom could put up with Darlene. Ever since our parents split up last March, it seemed as if Darlene had been punishing the whole family. Mom said that Darlene needed time to adjust. As far as I was concerned, Mom and Dad seemed a lot happier apart, but that didn't count for much with Darlene. Dad lived only two hours away, in San Diego, and she refused to see him. She wouldn't even talk to him on the phone.

"Don't you think Darlene's a pain, Ninja?" He was gnawing on the leather leash and trying to pull me into the gutter. Then he shook his head frantically with the leash still in his mouth and ran around me, wrapping my legs together.

"Ninja," I said. "Stop it!" I spun in the opposite direction, tripping as I tried to unravel myself. He tugged on the leash again with his teeth. Suddenly it snapped and Ninja dashed down the sidewalk.

"Get back here!" I screamed, untangling myself and chasing after him. "Ninja!" He ran back toward me with half the leash still dangling from his mouth. I tried to grab him, but he barked and ran away. "Come here!" I pleaded. He darted into the street. A car was coming.

"Hey, not so fast, little guy." A boy ran into the street from the opposite sidewalk and scooped Ninja up. The car passed a second later.

"Thank you! Thank you!" I called as I ran up to him. "Thanks so much!"

"No problem," he said. "Is Scruffy yours?"

"Yes," I said. "His name's Ninja."

"He looks more like a Scruffy to me," the boy said. I recognized him from our school bus. "Spike here," he said, and held out his free hand. "Who are you?"

"I'm Marci," I said, shaking his hand. "Don't you go to Franklin?"

"I sure do. I just started this year—the big seventh grade!"

"Me too," I said.

Ninja was busy chewing on Spike's fluorescent green T-shirt. Spike wore colorful Hawaiian print shorts, and his blond hair was cut short in a flattop. He's kind of cute, I thought. In a funny way.

"Your leash looks like it's shot," Spike said, taking off the mangled leather piece still hanging from Ninja's collar. "I have an extra leash at my house. Do you want to borrow it? I live right down the street. And I have a puppy too—part collie and part German shepherd. Scruffy might want to meet her."

"Sure," I said, following him down the road. He carried Ninja.

"So, how do you like Franklin?" he asked.

"It's all right," I said. "For school, I mean."

"Yeah. Actually, I really like it. There are thousands of people at Franklin, and I'm a people-watcher. And I'm working as an assistant editor for the school paper, which I love. I'm learning French, too. It's all pretty cool."

"I was thinking of taking Spanish next year," I said. A foreign language was a requirement in eighth and ninth grade. I was dreading it because I'd heard it was really hard.

"I think I'll take Spanish in high school," he said. "There are so many Spanish-speaking people around here, I think it'd be cool to be able to talk to them."

I'd never thought about language in that way. I was impressed.

"Hey, Scruffy, watch it. I like my shirt," Spike said. Ninja had already chewed a hole through the collar.

"I'll take him," I volunteered.

"Naw, he's just a baby. He doesn't know any better. Besides, we're here. C'mon." I followed Spike up a short driveway to a two-story adobe-style home. He walked into the attached garage. A bright-turquoise bike was locked to a beam in the corner. A half-put-together red mountain bike was tilted sideways on a bike stand. There were screwdrivers, wrenches, greasy rags, tire tubes and bike chains scattered all over the floor.

"Who's the cyclist in the family?" I asked.

"I am. I'm responsible for all of this mess," he said proudly. He walked over to the turquoise bike. "This is Primo," he said. "The love of my life. Primo, meet Marci."

I laughed. "Primo?"

"You know, like a prima ballerina," he said. "Only my bike's a guy."

"Nice to meet you, Primo," I said.

"We're going to win the Coastal Classic together," Spike said. "Aren't we, Primo?" He patted the bike.

"What's that?"

"It's a big race on February 15 up the Coast Highway. I've been in training already for a month."

Spike went over to the mountain bike. "And this is my newest purchase. It cost twenty-five dollars at a junkyard. I'm taking it apart and trying to rebuild it. This will be my cruiser. Do you ride?"

"Well, not really," I admitted. "I don't have a bike."

"Maybe when I finish fixing this one, you can use it and we can go for a ride," Spike said.

"That would be fun."

Ninja barked. "Oh, yeah. Your leash," Spike said. He dug a chain leash out of a drawer and attached it to Ninja's collar. "Try to chew through this, little guy."

"Thanks," I said.

"Wait here a second," Spike said. He put Ninja down and handed me the leash. He walked inside his house and returned a few minutes later with a fluffy brown-and-tan puppy in his arms.

"Marci, Scruffy, meet T-Bone."

"T-Bone? Where'd *that* name come from?"

"The first day I got her, she climbed onto the kitchen counter and ate our dinner, a T-bone steak."

"You're great with names," I said. "How'd you get the name Spike?"

Spike laughed and leaned his head toward me. "Feel my hair," he said.

The ends of his hair stuck straight up. I ran my hand across the top. It felt prickly. "Ouch," I joked. "A girl could cut herself."

"Exactly," Spike said. "Come on, I'll give you and Scruffy a ride home."

"On the bike? You're crazy!"

"I know, but it'll be fun." After he put T-Bone in the house he grabbed a backpack off one of the shelves, unlocked the bike and pushed it out to the driveway. He turned to me. "You ready?"

"I guess." I didn't feel ready.

Spike put Ninja inside his backpack, leaving an opening at the top. Ninja popped his head out and barked. Spike put the pack on his back. "Now you sit right here," he said, patting the bar in front of his seat.

I climbed on. "If I die, make sure Ninja gets home," I said. Spike laughed. Then he pushed off with his leg. The bike wobbled down Spike's driveway.

"Whoa!" I called, grabbing the handlebars.

"Hang on!" Spike steadied the bike and we rode up the street. Ninja yapped the whole way back to my house.

"Thanks for the ride," I said as I toppled off the bike.

"No problem," said Spike. "Listen, I'll be training

T-Bone soon. You want to get the two pups together for a session?"

"Sure."

"Great! I'll see you at school," he said, and rode away.

As I walked into the house the phone was ringing. "Marci, it's Pam," Darlene called. "Don't be long. Bill's calling soon."

I rolled my eyes. Bill phoned Darlene at least twice a day, usually right before dinner and again about eight at night. What on earth did they talk about?

I told Pam about Spike.

"I know who he is," she said. "Do you have a crush on him?"

"No," I said. "He's just fun to talk to."

"Okaaay," she said with that tone of voice that let me know she didn't believe me for a second. "So, have you come up with any ideas for our boyfriend mission?"

"No."

"Marci!" Darlene called. "Get off the phone!"

I ignored her. "What do you suppose Darlene and Bill talk about a hundred times a day?" I asked Pam.

"Only one way to find out."

I lowered my voice. "You mean, listen to them on the phone?" I had to admit, it was an interesting idea.

"Sure," said Pam. "Darlene always has a boyfriend. She's got to be an expert on the subject."

"But how can we do it without getting caught?"

"I saw in a movie once that if you unscrew the mouthpiece on the receiver of a phone, you can listen without being heard."

"What do you mean?" I asked. "My phone doesn't

have anything you can unscrew. The push-button pad is on the receiver and the mouthpiece is square."

"Maybe it just works on old phones," Pam said. "Hold on."

I waited about five minutes. "Pam, are you there?" I asked. "Pam, where are you?" I was about to hang up when she came back on.

"It works!" she crowed. "My parents have a phone they keep in the closet that doesn't have push buttons. I unscrewed the receiver and plugged it in, and I could hear you asking if I was there. Didn't you hear me answer?"

"No," I said.

"Awesome!" Pam said. "I'll bring my phone over tomorrow night and we'll intercept the eight o'clock call."

"It's a date."

3

At seven forty-five the next night Pam and I peeked out of my room, which was right between Darlene's and Timmy's. No one was in the hall. I checked downstairs. My mom was watching TV, and Timmy was asleep next to her. Darlene had a phone in her room, so she'd probably take the call in there.

We tiptoed into my mom's room at the end of the hall. Pam unscrewed the receiver on the phone she'd brought and plugged it into the wall in place of my mom's. Then we sat on the bed and waited. I had our notebook—a fresh one this time—ready.

Suddenly the phone rang. We both jumped. Then we started giggling so hard we couldn't stop.

"Shhh!" Pam finally managed to say. "The mission begins!" The phone stopped ringing after the third ring. Pam carefully picked up the receiver and held it to her ear. I pressed my head to hers so I could hear.

"Is Darlene there?" Bill asked.

"What do you mean, 'Is Darlene there?'" Darlene

snapped. Her voice sounded deep and raspy. "Bill, it's me."

"Wow, your voice has gotten worse since this afternoon. You sound really sexy when you're sick."

"Thanks," said Darlene sarcastically. "I wish I didn't have to feel sick to have a sexy voice."

Pam nudged me.

I wrote in our book:

DEEP VOICE IS SEXY. SHOULD WE TRY TO GET LARYNGITIS?

We listened intently. Bill and Darlene talked about their friend cheating on a test in school, about Darlene's math teacher giving an unfair test and about Bill's *A* on a history paper.

Then they talked some more—about Bill's best friend asking Darlene's friend out on a date, a party they'd heard about, how Bill's parents had been fighting and that it really bothered him. Darlene told Bill that she thought he'd been playing basketball too much and that they needed to spend more time together. "I'll try harder," he said.

Pam nudged me. "Did you get that?" she whispered.

"Shhh!" I hissed. I was furiously trying to write everything down.

"Do you want to play volleyball after school tomorrow?" Bill asked Darlene.

"Let me see how I feel," she said. "Besides my throat hurting, I just got my period and I've got cramps."

Pam grabbed my arm. My mouth dropped open and I looked at her in horror. How could Darlene *say* that to him? I thought. He's a boy!

I scribbled madly in the book, at the same time keeping my ear pressed to the phone so I wouldn't miss anything.

"Well, take it easy this week and let's make plans for Saturday," Bill said. "How about going to see the new Michael J. Fox movie?"

"Yeah. I'm dying to see that," Darlene said. "Let's have dinner at the Flamingo Café before the show."

"Okay," Bill agreed. "It's a date."

"Super," Darlene said. "I'll see you tomorrow."

They hung up. So did we. Pam flopped back on the bed.

"Did you hear that?" she asked, amazed.

"I heard it!"

"I can't believe she talked about that stuff with a *boy*!" said Pam. "I mean, they covered everything! It sounded like a conversation that you and I would have—with each other! Of course, we don't talk about our periods because we haven't gotten them yet."

"Look at all these notes," I said, flipping through six pages of scribbles. "What a mess!"

"Let's make a list of topics they discussed," Pam suggested.

I wrote at the top of a new page:

PHONE TOPICS
1. SCHOOL——FRIENDS, SCHOOLWORK, TEACHERS
2. GOSSIP——FRIENDS DATING, PARTIES
3. FAMILY——PROBLEMS
4. RELATIONSHIP——TIME SPENT TOGETHER
5. PERSONAL——BEING SICK, HAVING PERIOD!!!
6. SOCIAL——PLANNING DATES

The phone rang. We both jumped and I stifled a scream. The phone was in pieces. Pam scrambled to unplug her phone. I grabbed my mom's phone and handed it to her.

"Marci, it's for you!" Darlene called.

"Unplug it!" I told Pam.

"I'm trying! I'm trying!"

"Marci? Did you hear me?" Darlene called. She started coming down the hall.

"Yes!" I yelled. "Just a second!" Pam climbed over me and plugged in my mom's phone. Then she stuffed her phone into her backpack.

"Ready," she whispered.

I picked up the phone. "Hello?"

"Hey, Marci. Spike here."

"Hi," I said. "What's up?"

Pam hit my arm.

"Who is it?" she whispered.

I pushed her away. "Spike," I mouthed. She put her ear next to mine.

"I called to see if you wanted to come over with Scruffy on Sunday. I'm going to train T-Bone."

"That sounds great," I said.

Pam picked up our book and pointed to the list of phone topics. I pushed her away again.

"What time's good for you?" Spike asked.

"It doesn't matter," I said. "Just not too early."

"How's noon? That way I can go for a ride in the morning."

"Okay," I said. Pam pushed the notebook into my face again and mouthed the words "Go for it!" I looked at the list.

"How's school?" I blurted out.

"Pretty good," Spike said. "The newspaper is taking up a lot of my time. I'm in charge of choosing the stories this month."

"Have you picked them yet?"

"For this week," he said. "But I'm clueless for next week. It's a lot of work."

"Sure sounds like it."

Pam pointed to the word GOSSIP on the list. I shook my head. Then she pointed to PERSONAL.

"Tell him you have your period," she whispered, and burst into laughter. I covered the receiver.

"Stop it," I whispered.

"What?" Spike asked.

"Nothing," I said, scowling at Pam. She giggled.

"Well, listen," Spike said. "T-Bone's chewing a hole in our rug, so I better go."

"Maybe you better start the training session earlier," I kidded.

"Really," he said. "So, if I don't see you at school, just come over on Sunday, okay?"

"Okay. See ya." I hung up.

Pam applauded. I threw a pillow at her.

"You have a date," she teased.

"It's not a date," I protested. "And you are a pain in the neck!"

"But a brilliant pain in the neck. I've figured out our next move."

"What?" I asked.

"We should have dinner at the Flamingo Café and go to the movies Saturday night. That way we can watch Darlene and Bill in action."

"I like it. I like it," I said. "But what if they see us?"

"It's a free country. We can go where we want."

"Great idea!"

"I told you I was brilliant," she said.

"And conceited."

This time she threw the pillow at me.

"We'd like to sit in the back, please," said Pam to the restaurant hostess. It was Saturday night and we were at the Flamingo Café.

She seated us in the corner, where we were practically hidden by a giant plastic pink flamingo. As soon as we sat down I pulled out our notebook and a pen from my purse.

"I'm ready," I announced. "Let's eat!"

"Marci, we're on a mission. You can't eat. You have to watch the door. I can't see a thing because that stupid pink flamingo's in my way."

I glanced quickly over my shoulder. She was right. The dumb bird blocked my view, too. The only way I'd be able to see anything was if I got on my knees and peered over the booth divider behind me. "Okay, I'll watch. But it's only six thirty—Darlene and Bill probably won't turn up for a while, and I'm hungry."

We ordered chef's salads and Diet Cokes.

"Hey, better get ready," Pam whispered, trying to peer around the bird. "I think someone just came in."

I got up on my knees to get a view of the doorway. "Oh, my God!" I sat down with a flop.

"What? What?" asked Pam.

"It's TDH!" That was our nickname for Patrick Bell, who was definitely tall, dark and handsome. He was also a star jock—one of the best players on Franklin Junior High's varsity volleyball team. He was in eighth grade. I'd never actually met him, but I saw him around school a lot. And I could always hope. "He's with another guy from the volleyball team and they're walking straight toward us!"

Pam held her hand to her forehead and pretended she was fainting.

"Quit it! They'll see you," I begged. Pam just laughed.

"This is fine," I heard one of them saying to the hostess as they slid into the booth behind me. Patrick and I were back to back—only the divider separated us!

"Look again. Someone else came in," said Pam. "I think it may be Darlene and Bill."

I sat up to peek over the seat. Patrick turned around at the same time and looked straight into my eyes!

"Hello," he said.

"Hi," I squeaked, and sat back down.

"Well?" Pam asked.

"He's *so* cute!" I whispered.

"Marci, you're supposed to be looking for Darlene. Was that her?"

"Oh. I don't know," I whispered. "I panicked when TDH looked at me."

"Flirting again?" She grinned at me.

"I am not!"

"Oh, yes you are," she said, a little louder.

"Oh, yes you are what?" asked a male voice. I looked

over my shoulder. Patrick was peering into our booth. How much had he heard? I turned red.

"Oh, yes you are going to the movie," Pam explained. "Marci couldn't decide if she wanted to go to the movie or not."

That's what I love about Pam. No matter how embarrassing a situation is, she can always come up with something to say.

"Marci, of course you should go to the movie," said Patrick. He smiled at me and two dimples appeared. I blushed again. "We're going," he said. "It's supposed to be a great flick."

"That's what I was telling her," Pam added, kicking me under the table.

"I guess I'll go then," I said. I looked at Patrick. He was still smiling.

"Good choice," Patrick's friend agreed. He was husky, with blond hair parted on the side and freckles. He was pretty cute too, I thought, but Patrick . . .

"Oh no!" Pam gasped, and gave me a quick nudge.

"What?"

"It's Darlene!"

I ducked down.

"Who's Darlene?" asked Patrick.

"Darlene is Marci's sister," Pam said.

If she tells them the truth, I'll die, I thought.

"She's been lying and getting in trouble at home lately. Marci's mom wanted us to sort of spy on her to make sure she went where she said she was going."

"Right," I said. "We can't let her see us." I wondered if they believed a word we were saying.

"No problem," said Patrick. His chocolate-brown eyes looked into mine. "We'll be your spies."

"Yeah," said the other guy. "I'll be Agent 35 and this'll be Agent 44. Those are our team numbers."

"What team?" Pam asked innocently.

"Franklin volleyball," said Patrick. "Varsity."

"We go to Franklin," I said.

"I thought you looked familiar. I'm Patrick."

I look familiar? I thought. That means he's noticed me! I couldn't speak. There was a moment of silence. Then Pam said, "I'm Pam." She kicked me under the table again.

"I'm Marci," I finally said.

"And this is Tony," Patrick said.

"Your sister's sitting in the front of the restaurant," Tony reported.

"Thanks, Agent 35," Pam said.

The waitress arrived with our food.

"Well, we'll let you eat now," said Patrick. "But don't worry, we'll keep you posted."

"Thanks." I smiled at them as they settled back into their booth.

Pam and I looked at each other.

"Where did you come up with that story?" I whispered.

"I don't know," she said. "It just came out of my mouth."

Tony poked his head over the seat. "They're holding hands across the table," he reported, and then popped back down.

"I think I'm in love!" Pam whispered. "Isn't he awesome?"

"TDH?"

"No. The other one," she whispered. "Let's call him GE—for his beautiful green eyes!"

I hadn't noticed Tony's eyes. I had been too busy staring at Patrick. I was relieved that Pam liked Tony. I would have hated for us to have a crush on the same guy.

By the time we were finished with dinner, Patrick and Tony had informed us that Darlene was eating pasta and Bill was having a burger. They had shared a salad.

"Wait," Tony said. "Yes, it's true. Darlene is putting Parmesan cheese on her pasta."

"You guys are crazy!" Pam said.

"You got it!" said Patrick. "We're wild and crazy guys."

Before we knew it, it was seven forty-five—time for the movie. We paid our bill.

"Hey, they're getting ready to go," said Tony. "Darlene's putting on her black jacket. Now Bill's putting on his jean jacket. They're walking to the door. They're walking out the door. They're gone." He fell back into his seat.

"So, now what?" Patrick asked.

"Now," said Pam, "we have to follow them to the movie."

"Well, why don't the four of us go together?" Patrick suggested.

I must be dreaming, I thought.

"After all," added Tony, "what would you do without your spies?"

We got up and walked single file to the door. Patrick led the way, and I was right behind him.

"Wait," he said, halting suddenly. I didn't stop in time,

and my face landed right between Patrick's shoulder blades. All four of us burst into laughter.

Finally Patrick opened the door. "Let me see if your sister's gone, first." He peeked outside. "All clear," he reported.

We managed to get into the theater without being spotted by Darlene and Bill. While Tony and Patrick went to stand in the candy line, Pam and I ran to the bathroom.

"Oh, my God," I said when we were inside. "Can you believe this?"

"I'm numb," said Pam. She took out her brush and fixed her hair. I did the same.

"Are we on a date or what?" I asked.

"I don't know," she said. "But we better get out there before we lose them."

We scurried out of the bathroom and hid behind a giant cardboard cutout of a Kung Fu man. I couldn't see my sister anywhere. Patrick and Tony were still in line.

"Hey, what are you doing here?" someone said. I turned around. It was Darlene!

"We came to the movies," I said. "Is that okay with you?"

"Are you here alone?"

"Yes," Pam and I said in unison.

"We brought you some M&Ms," said Tony as he walked over. He looked at Darlene and then back at us. Patrick was right behind him. I blushed furiously. Pam just smiled.

"Hi. I'm Darlene, Marci's sister."

"Hi, Darlene. I'm Tony."

"Darlene, was it?" said Patrick. "Very nice to meet you. I'm Patrick."

Bill walked up and Darlene introduced him.

"Well, have fun," Darlene said. "Alone, huh?" she whispered to me as she left.

The second Darlene and Bill were out of sight Tony said, "We leave you for five seconds and you get caught."

"You were supposed to warn us," said Pam.

"That's right," I teased. "You're fired."

"Can we still sit together?" asked Tony.

"I suppose so," Pam said airily.

As we were walking into the theater three guys stopped Patrick and Tony and started discussing volleyball. No one introduced us. I picked at the M&Ms, crossed my arms, uncrossed them. Pam fidgeted next to me. The guys kept talking.

"We better go get seats," Pam finally said.

"Yeah," I agreed.

"Save us a couple," said Patrick.

"I'll go with the girls," said Tony.

Pam and I sat next to each other and Tony sat on the outside next to Pam. When Patrick joined us, he sat next to Tony. They kept cracking jokes and laughing during the movie. Pam and I couldn't help laughing too.

When the movie was over, the four of us walked outside together. I couldn't think of anything to say.

"Well, it was really fun meeting you," said Tony. "Even though we failed as your spies." He looked at Pam. "Do you think I could call you sometime?" he asked.

I pretended not to hear. I knew Pam must be dying. She told him her number. He said he'd remember it.

I looked at Patrick and tried smiling. I didn't know

what to do with my hands, so I crossed them in front of me. I felt totally awkward.

"Maybe we could make it a foursome," Patrick said to me.

My heart was pounding. "Sure," I said. "That would be fun."

"Why don't you write down your number for me," he said. "I don't have a great memory."

I wrote my number down and handed the paper to Patrick. Then I heard my name being called. Pam's father had just stopped the car in front of the theater to pick us up.

"We'll see you at school," Pam said to Tony and Patrick.

"Bye," they said together.

"See ya," I said. We walked to the car and both climbed in the front seat. I felt like I was going to burst.

We drove away.

"How was the movie?" Pam's dad asked.

"Movie? What movie? Did we just see a movie?" Pam asked, holding her hands over her heart and falling onto me.

5

"Ring!" I commanded the phone.

It was nine on Sunday night and I hadn't left the house all day. What if Patrick called and I wasn't home? Worse, what if Timmy answered and said something embarrassing? I had even canceled the puppy-training session with Spike. Now I felt stupid.

I dialed Pam's number. She picked it up on the first ring.

"It's just me," I said.

"Oh, hi." I could tell that Tony hadn't called either.

"I'm giving up. I don't think he'll ever call."

"I'm giving up too." She sighed. "We should have given them one number so we could wait together."

"I agree. I'm going to sleep."

"Me too," said Pam. We hung up.

The next day at school I looked for Patrick. A part of me really wanted to see him, but another part of me didn't. What if he didn't even recognize me?

Pam and I met at our usual table for lunch.

"I saw Tony talking to a really cute girl this morning," she announced mournfully.

"Did he see you?"

"No way. He was right on the path to my class, so I went all the way around the D building to avoid running into him."

"That's great!" I said. "We sit home all day and wait for the guys to call and then we avoid them at school."

"I guess that *is* pretty silly."

"I think we should forget about them. They're probably not our types anyway."

"What *are* our types?" Pam asked.

"I don't know."

"Let's make a list. Do you have our book?"

I searched my pack, but it wasn't there. I pulled out my science notebook—that would have to do for now.

By the end of lunch we had figured out everything we wanted in a boyfriend. I read the list to Pam.

1. CUTE
2. ATHLETIC
3. POPULAR
4. FUNNY
5. NICE

"Uh-oh," Pam said.

"What?"

"Those traits fit Tony perfectly."

"And Patrick," I added.

"It's hopeless!" Pam grumbled as we parted for class. "We're never going to forget about them!"

When I got home that afternoon, Darlene was sitting on the couch.

"Hi," I said. She stood up and glared at me.

"Yes?" I asked. "What's your problem?"

"The question is, what's *your* problem?" Darlene said furiously. She held up my secret book. "How dare you listen in on my phone conversations and try to follow me!"

"Where did you find that? Why were you snooping through my things?"

"I didn't have to snoop through anything. The book was lying on the table in the living room. I was just looking for a piece of paper and I found it."

How could I have been so stupid? I thought. "I'm sorry," I said meekly. "I just wanted to know how to talk to boys on the phone."

"Well, why didn't you just ask?"

"I don't know," I said. "You always know what to do around boys. I never do. But I felt dumb asking. Besides, you've been in such a horrible mood lately. I never want to talk to you anymore."

"I haven't been in a horrible mood," she snapped.

"Yes, you have—ever since Dad moved out."

"Well, that's Dad's fault. He destroyed our family."

"No, he didn't. Mom and Dad were miserable together. They're both happier apart. You should be too."

Darlene didn't answer.

"Why don't you just give him a chance?" I asked.

Darlene sighed and stared at the ceiling. "I need to think about it."

"It would really mean a lot to him."

"I'll make you a deal," Darlene said. "I'll try to be nicer to Dad if you'll stop spying."

"It's a deal."

"If you want advice, just ask," she added.

"Thanks. Can I start now?"

"Sure. Shoot."

"Remember that guy you met at the movie theater? The cute one named Patrick?"

"Yes."

"Well, he said he'd call me and he hasn't."

"Marci, it's only Monday."

The phone rang. My heart skipped a beat. I reached over to answer it, but Darlene blocked me.

"Rule number one," she said. "Let the phone ring at least twice before answering it. You don't want to seem overanxious."

She picked up the phone after the second ring. "Hello," she said. "Yes, she is. Just a minute." Darlene mouthed that it was a boy. I reached for the phone. She pulled it away.

"Marci!" she called loudly. I was standing eight inches away from her. "It's for you!"

I giggled. Darlene handed me the phone.

"Hello."

"Hi, Marci," a male voice said. "Spike here."

"Oh, hi," I said, trying to hide my disappointment. Darlene looked at me questioningly. I shook my head.

"Listen," Spike said. "I'm right in the middle of a deadline and my typewriter broke. Do you have one I could borrow?"

"I'll ask," I said. "Darlene, can Spike borrow your typewriter?"

"Sure."

"You can borrow my sister's," I told him.

"Great," Spike said. "I'll ride Primo over right now. See ya in a few."

We hung up. The phone rang again. I looked at Darlene. I waited for two rings and then answered it.

"He called! He called! He called!" Pam screamed. "Tony really called!"

"That's great!" I tried to sound excited.

"He asked me on a date for Saturday night! Can you believe it? A real date!" Pam was talking so fast her words slurred together. "Marci, I'm so excited. What am I going to wear? Where do you think he'll take me? How can I wait until Saturday? What if I see him at school?"

"Whoa, girl. Slow down!" I said.

"I'm sorry. I'll be fine. But Marci, I can't believe he called. We only talked for a few minutes, but that's all right. Isn't it? He still asked me out."

"That's great," I said again. But all the time I was thinking, Why hasn't Patrick called me? The way things were going for Pam, she was sure to have a boyfriend by Valentine's Day. With my luck, I wasn't even going to have a date.

"I'll see you tomorrow at the bus stop," she bubbled. "I'll tell you all the details then."

"Congratulations!" I said. "See ya."

Darlene looked at me sympathetically as I hung up.

"What's wrong with me?" I asked her.

"Nothing's wrong with you," she said softly. "Be patient."

"Sure."

Spike arrived a few minutes later and picked up the typewriter. He handed Darlene a bag of peanut butter cookies. "Rental fee," he said, darting out the door.

Patrick never called.

"No, really," insisted Pam. "It's true. Guys only care about looks."

We were halfway through lunch on Tuesday.

"Then how come so many ugly girls have boy-friends?" I asked.

That's when Spike showed up.

"So, how'd it go last night?" I asked him.

"I was up all night," he said. "I still need one more story for this week and something for next week. Any suggestions?"

"How about, What do boys like in girls?" Pam offered.

"I like it," Spike said eagerly.

"I was kidding," Pam said.

"Do you think you two could do the story? Of course, you'd have to write what girls like in boys also."

"Spike, are you crazy?" I asked.

"I was just kidding," Pam repeated. "How would we know something like that?"

"I'm sure there are books on the subject." Spike was on a roll. "Or you could interview kids at school."

"No way," I said.

"It'll be a great story," he said, ignoring our protests. "Can you start today?"

Pam and I looked at each other. "No way," we exclaimed in unison.

But Spike wouldn't take no for an answer. Before we knew it, he'd dragged us over to the newspaper office to introduce us to Mr. Thompson, the faculty adviser. Mr. Thompson loved the idea.

"I'm not asking anyone our age," I warned Pam when we left. "It's bad enough that we got conned into doing the story, but I don't want anyone to know we did it."

"Me neither," Pam agreed. "We better stick to the library."

"Across town," I added.

"Miles and miles across town," Pam said.

"In another state."

A library twenty minutes from home was the farthest we got. I typed *relationships* on the computer index keyboard. Then *boys, girls, romance, dating, flirting.* Pam wrote down the call numbers of the books that sounded the most interesting.

It took us an hour to find a quarter of the books on our list. We ended up with *Ten Quick Ways to Get a Date, Unlucky at Love?, Who's Your Perfect Mate?, What Are Men Looking For?, How to Find Your Match, The Boyfriend Hunt,* and *How to Make Yourself Attractive.*

We found an empty table and began to read.

"Listen to this," I whispered. " 'Do you feel as though you're the only one not in love?' "

"Yes," Pam answered.

" 'Are all of your friends married or engaged?' "

"No," she said.

"You're supposed to answer yes," I told her.

"Okay. Yes."

" 'You're not alone,' " I continued. " 'There are many other women who have the same fears, feel the same loneliness.' "

"That's depressing!" Pam said. "My book's much more exciting. Listen: 'There are many problems when relationships are based only on sex.' "

"Pam, we've barely *kissed* anyone," I whispered, embarrassed.

"So, we need to know what lies ahead."

I shook my head and continued reading my book. "This sounds like us. 'Many women assume there's something wrong with them if they're not dating. They try to change themselves so they become more attractive to men.' "

"It *does* sound like us. . . ." Pam said.

"Do you suppose other kids our age do that too?" I asked.

"I don't know. How could we find out?" Pam asked.

"Maybe we could write up a questionnaire," I suggested. "Wouldn't that be fun? Just like in *Sassy* magazine."

"I love it!" Pam declared. "Do you think Spike would put it in the paper instead of an article?"

"I don't know. Let's write down all the questions we can think of and ask him tomorrow."

"Great."

I opened another book and started reading. Then I heard a ruffling noise and looked up. Through the stack of books in front of me I saw a guy's face. He had blue eyes and was at least eighteen. Two guys joined him, and they sat down across from us.

"Looking for a date?" the blue-eyed one said, and snickered. The other guys laughed. They were staring at our books.

I smiled nervously. I didn't know what else to do. Pam jumped in immediately with our newspaper explanation. Even though it was the truth, I felt really stupid. I wondered if they believed us.

One of the guys picked up *How to Find Your Match*.

"Are *you* looking for a date?" I teased. We all laughed.

Five minutes later Pam and I checked out a few books and left. On our way home we decided that we would have to write all our findings into our secret book. It was great information and might help us in our boyfriend quest.

When I got home, Darlene was in the kitchen.

"Well, did Patrick call?" I asked her. She shook her head.

"He's never going to call," I complained. "And I'm *never* going to get a date to the Valentine's Day dance."

"Now, that's not true, Marci," she said. "Maybe he's shy."

"TDH? I don't think so! He just doesn't like me."

"Marci, boys can be shy too," she insisted.

"I know, I know. I've been reading all about it."

"So why don't you do something about it?"

"Like what?"

"Get involved in something he's interested in. Does

he belong to a club at school? I met Bill at a ski club meeting."

"All I know is he plays volleyball," I said.

"Can you join the pep squad?"

"I doubt it."

"Well, just find out what he's interested in and let me know. We'll come up with something."

"Okay."

7

The questionnaire idea was a hit with Spike and Mr. Thompson. They wanted to put it in the next issue, which meant it had to be finished by Friday. It was already Wednesday. Mr. Thompson had said he had a free fifth period Thursday and he'd write us notes to get out of class so he could help us. Pam had a test, so she didn't even ask. I had P.E.

After school that day I went to find Coach Stratton, my P.E. teacher. He was also the volleyball coach. I knew there was a chance that I'd run into Patrick.

I was both relieved and disappointed when I found the coach alone in his office.

"That's fine," he said when I asked him about skipping class. "And since you're going to be at the paper office anyway, can I ask you a favor?"

"Sure," I said.

"Could you ask Thompson to put a note in the paper for me?" I nodded. He scribbled something onto a piece of paper and handed it to me. "The girl who's been keeping statistics at the volleyball games had to drop

♥ 41 ♥

out," he said. "There's a game in a couple of days and I have no one to help me."

A light bulb went off in my head, but I ignored it.

"Thanks, Marci," the coach said.

"No problem," I answered, and started walking toward the door.

I kept hearing Darlene's voice saying, "Get involved with something Patrick's interested in." I turned back.

"Excuse me," I said. I couldn't believe I was doing this. "Do you think I could do the statistics for you?"

"Of course," Coach Stratton said. "Do you have the time?"

"Well, yeah," I said. Then I started to feel nervous. "What if I get my friend Pam to help? Then if one of us has too much work, the other can do it. You won't be left without help."

"Perfect," he said. "There's a game on Monday. Be here at three that day so I can explain the rules before the game."

"Great," I said. "Bye." I ran all the way to the school bus.

"You what?" Pam screeched happily when I told her the news. Several people on the bus turned around.

"Shhh!"

"I can't believe it!" she whispered. "You and me and the whole team! Especially TDH and GE."

Pam talked about Tony all the way to my house. Since we planned to work with Spike on the questionnaire all night, I collected my *Sassy* magazines and Darlene's *Mademoiselle*s so we could see how the big magazines wrote questionnaires. Spike arrived at four with a book on teenage relationships.

The three of us sat in a puddle of books, magazines

and papers on my living room floor. Timmy sat in the middle. He thought we were playing some sort of game. My mom made chicken and salad for dinner, and then we had ice cream sundaes.

My sundae was all chocolate. Pam had vanilla with hot fudge. Spike filled his bowl with three scoops of ice cream, fudge, nuts, cherries and sprinkles.

"You sure can eat a lot for a skinny guy," I teased.

"Hey, who are you calling skinny? I'm just trim."

"Okay. Okay," I said. "You sure eat a lot for a trim guy."

"Much better," he said.

"Hey, you two," Pam called to Spike and me from the living room. "This book is great. Come here and listen to this."

We joined her on the couch. " 'One of the biggest problems with teens is that many are too concerned with appearance and popularity,' " she read. " 'Ask yourself why you're interested in a boy or girl. Do you have common interests? Will you have anything to talk about? If you can overcome your attraction to looks and popularity, there may be someone who is a much better match for you. Maybe that someone is in your math class, the soccer club, student council. Someone you hadn't noticed before. Someone who can be a friend as much as a romantic interest. Someone more accessible.' "

"Maybe that's our problem, Marci," Pam whispered to me while Spike started flipping through some magazines. "Do you think we're caught up in this popularity thing? Do you think that Patrick and Tony are really jerks underneath? Now I'm panicked about my date."

"Oh, stop worrying," I said. "You're going to have a

great time. You two will have plenty to talk about. As for Patrick, I don't think the problem is that he's a jerk. I just think he has a million girls after him and I don't stand a chance."

"Just wait until the game on Monday," Pam said.

"What's going on?" Spike cut in. "I'm feeling left out."

"Sorry, Spike," I said. "Just girl talk."

"Yeah, but this is the kind of stuff we want to put in the questionnaire," he said. Then he looked at me. "Besides, how come I didn't know you liked anyone?"

Oh no! He overheard! I smiled nervously and shrugged. I wasn't used to talking about crushes in front of boys. Even though it was only Spike, I still felt weird. Did he really expect me to tell him about Patrick? I looked at Spike. He was staring at the rug.

I picked up *Unlucky at Love?* and buried my face in it. I read: "To have a good relationship, both parties must work hard at it." Tell me about it, I thought.

"Being open and honest about what you're feeling will help build a strong relationship." I wasn't sure how I could work on building my relationship with Patrick. We had only talked once.

"People need to be happy with themselves before a relationship can work." If I lost ten pounds, jogged a lot and grew boobs, I'd be happy with myself, I thought. And maybe then Patrick would call me.

"But don't change for someone else," the book continued. "Change for yourself."

"Hey, this is great!" called Pam. "My book says that even people our parents' age get nervous when they talk to someone they're attracted to. Can you imagine our parents acting like teenagers?"

"I think they're referring to singles," said Spike. "I doubt my mom gets nervous around my dad."

"I can't think about my parents being attracted to other people," I said. "That's too weird."

"What about you, Spike?" Pam asked. "Do you get nervous around a girl you have a crush on?"

"Well, first of all, boys don't get *crushes,*" he replied. "We may like a girl, but we don't get a *crush.*"

"You didn't answer the question," I pointed out.

Spike blushed. "Well, yes," he admitted. "I get nervous."

"What do you do if you want to talk to a girl, but you're nervous?" Pam asked.

"I probably wouldn't talk to her," Spike said. "Or if I did, I would try to make it look like it was unplanned. Hey, what is this—the third degree? What about you two?"

"I would run all the way around the D building to avoid him," Pam declared.

"And I would pretend that I didn't see him, probably," I told him.

"What are you afraid would happen?" Spike asked me.

"I don't know. Maybe that I wouldn't know what to say." I couldn't believe I was admitting this to a boy.

"I would be afraid that he didn't like me and I was just making a fool of myself," Pam confessed.

"What about you?" I asked Spike.

"I guess I would just be afraid the girl didn't like me."

"You mean boys think that way too?" I was amazed.

"Sure. Well, maybe not the popular ones."

"Like our soon-to-be boyfriends?" Pam asked, grinning.

"So, you don't think volleyball studs like Patrick and Tony could be insecure too?" I asked Spike.

"I don't know," he said. "Guys don't really talk about things like that. Besides, I don't even know Patrick and Tony. But I'm sure they're insecure about something."

"Listen to this," said Pam, reading from the book she was holding. " 'All people go through a time when they're afraid of not being loved, of being the only one without a partner. Each person has his or her own insecurity. Some think they're too fat, too skinny, too tall or too short. Others believe they're not smart enough or not athletic enough. Some are afraid of carrying on a conversation, or tripping when they walk. Everyone has something about which they're insecure.' "

"What's your biggest insecurity?" I asked Spike.

He looked away. "Being too skinny," he mumbled.

I thought about what I'd said to him in the kitchen. I felt bad, and it must have showed.

He smiled. "Don't worry about it. What's *your* biggest insecurity?" he asked me.

I'm too fat, I thought. And not pretty enough, and flat-chested, and too shy. "That I'm not pretty," I said finally. It seemed the easiest to admit.

"You're very pretty," Spike said. I blushed.

"I agree," said Pam. "But I'm ditto on that insecurity."

"Don't be silly, Pam. You're beautiful," I told her.

And so the evening went on. We read, talked, laughed and took notes until nine thirty. It was fun. I had never discussed such intimate subjects with a boy. We talked about going on dates. None of us had really experienced what we considered to be a *real* date. That was, a preplanned evening or day together. We even discussed kissing. Spike said he'd kissed a few girls, but he was always nervous at first. Pam and I said that we hadn't kissed much. I had kissed Dave once, but it was really quick. Pam had kissed a guy when we were in sixth grade.

After we analyzed all our research, we put together a first draft of the questionnaire. Although it still needed work, I thought it sounded good. By the time Pam and Spike left at eleven, I was exhausted.

As I drifted off to sleep, I thought how strange it was talking about dating and kissing and boyfriends with Spike. He was different from other boys. I found myself wishing that Patrick were more like him.

After one period of Mr. Thompson's editing, our questionnaire was ready for print. The finished product was polished and concise. We had signed it "By L. V. Hunt." Pam and I had come up with the pseudonym last night. It stood for Love Hunt, but of course we were the only ones who knew that.

After school I rushed to the bus stop. I couldn't wait to tell Pam how well the questionnaire had turned out. She didn't show up until the bus was about to leave.

"I just saw Tony," she cooed when she sat down. "He's so cute!"

"What did he say?" I asked. I wished I could share her excitement, but every time she mentioned Tony, it made me think of Patrick.

"We talked about lots of things," she said. "Like classes and volleyball. I told him we were going to be working at the games."

"And?"

"He said he thought it was great. And that he couldn't wait till Saturday night." She fell onto me with a sigh.

"Get up, you big ham." I pushed her off of me. "Did he say anything about Patrick?"

"No. But I didn't ask, and we were talking about other things. You know how it is."

"Sure," I said. But I was feeling left out. It was sort of like Pam had deserted me.

"So, what's up with the questionnaire?" she asked, changing the subject. Maybe she sensed that I was upset.

"It's going to be in the paper tomorrow," I told her. "And it came out great! Mr. Thompson said he's putting it on the front page."

"Wow!" Pam exclaimed. Still, I noticed she had been scribbling Tony's name all over her notebook.

"Tell me, what are you going to wear on Saturday?" I asked. I knew she was dying to talk about it.

She launched into a long list of all her clothes. For the rest of the ride we talked about skirts, sweaters, shirts, pants and Tony.

When I got home, Darlene was on the phone. "I have this paper that I've been working on in English that's really hard," she was saying. "Bill's been helping me a lot. . . . Yes, he's fine. . . . Everything's super. . . . Sure, you can meet him sometime. . . . Well, Marci just walked in. Do you want to talk to her?"

Darlene looked at me. "It's Dad," she said.

My mouth dropped open. Darlene smiled. This was the first time she'd talked to him since he moved out of the house! I took the phone.

"Hi, sweetheart." Dad's voice quivered with emotion. He was obviously in as much shock as I was. "I think we just jumped over a major hurdle with that sister of yours."

"No kidding," I replied.

After I hung up with Dad, I ran upstairs into Darlene's room. She was sitting on her bed.

"Thanks," I said. Darlene looked at me with tears in her eyes. I hugged her.

After dinner Darlene and I sat in her room talking until midnight. I told her everything I'd been feeling about Patrick. And about Pam and Tony. She told me I should be patient with Patrick and I shouldn't be angry with Pam. She said dating was new to Pam and I should let her enjoy the excitement. I knew she was right.

Then Darlene told me that she was really in love with Bill. She said she felt different with him than she had with any of her other boyfriends. I asked her what it felt like to be in love. She said that she felt as though she never wanted to be apart from Bill, that she thought about him constantly. She said she had never been happier.

I went to sleep that night thinking about what Darlene had said about love. Would I ever feel that way?

By the time Pam and I got to homeroom the next day, all the kids were reading our questionnaire. It was on the front page of the newspaper.

An Inside Look at Yourself—Relationships and Teens

1. Age___ 2. Grade___ 3. Sex (m/f)___

4. Rate yourself from 1–10 (10 being highest) in each of the following categories:

___Looks   ___Intelligence
___Reliability   ___Thoughtfulness
___Popularity   ___Confidence
___Sense of humor   ___Good listener
___Friendliness   ___Talents and interests
___Honesty   ___Other_____

5. When do you feel most self-conscious?

6. How good a friend are you? Rate yourself from 1–10:

__Reliable (Do you call when you say you will?)

__Thoughtful (Do you remember your friend's birthday?)

__Loyal (Would you stand up for your friend in a crowd?)

__Honest (Would you tell a friend that you think what he/she is doing is wrong?)

__Good listener (Do you really pay attention when your friend is talking?)

7. How popular do you think you are (1–10)?__

8. How comfortable are you talking to members of the opposite sex (1–10)? Friends__ Crushes__

9. At what age do you think people should start dating?

10. How would you let someone of the opposite sex know that you liked him/her?

11. How would you feel if someone you liked called you?

12. Have you ever been on a date? (If not, skip to question 14.)

13. Where did you go and how did you get there?

14. Where would you most like to go on a date? Why?

15. Where would you least like to go on a date? Why?

16. What makes you most nervous about going on a date?

17. What makes someone a boyfriend/girlfriend?

18. Have you ever had a boyfriend/girlfriend?

19. Do you have a boyfriend/girlfriend now? (If not, skip to question 24.)

20. How long have you been going together?

21. What do you like most about having a boyfriend/girlfriend?

22. What do you dislike most about having one?

23. How comfortable are you with that person (1–10)?—

24. If you don't have a steady relationship, would you like to have one? Why or why not?

25. Is there anything that makes you nervous about having a boyfriend/girlfriend?

26. What percentage of kids in this school do you think have boyfriends/girlfriends?

27. Have you ever been in love?

28. What would you look for in a boyfriend/girlfriend? Rate each category from 1–10 and circle the three most important.

    __Looks   __Intelligence
    __Reliability   __Thoughtfulness
    __Popularity   __Confidence
    __Sense of humor   __Good listener
    __Friendliness   __Talents and interests
    __Honesty   __Other_____

29. How honestly have you answered these questions (1–10)?__

"Can you believe it?" Pam whispered to me. I shook my head.

"How popular are *you*?" a guy sitting next to me asked his friend. They laughed.

"I wonder who L. V. Hunt is?" a girl asked Pam. I blushed. Pam smiled and shrugged her shoulders.

Just as Pam and I were about to part for class, Spike ran up and grabbed me. He lifted me in the air and twirled me around.

"It's a success! It's a success!" he yelled.

"Shhh!"

"No way! I'm in a great mood. Thompson's psyched! I'm psyched! What a fantastic day!"

"You're a madman!"

"Well, this madman wants to celebrate with you two madwomen! What do you say—dinner Saturday night? I'll cook."

"I can't make it," said Pam. "I have a date."

He turned to me. "Well, Madwoman Number One? What do you say?"

"Sounds good to me."

"What about this?" Pam turned around in a black mini-skirt, pink sweater and black tights.

"Too much black," I decided. "Try your jeans on again. With your lavender sweater."

"Oh, Marci, I'm sooo nervous," Pam said, squeezing out of the skirt. "Now, what did Darlene say?"

I picked up our secret book. I had asked Darlene to give us some dating tips before I left for Pam's house that night. I read:

1. DRESS NICELY, BUT COMFORTABLY. YOU DON'T WANT TO INTIMIDATE YOUR DATE. AND DRESSING CASUALLY WILL MAKE YOU FEEL MORE RELAXED ALSO.

"That's what Cathy told us too, remember?" Pam reminded me.

"Yes. But there's more."

2. DON'T EXPECT YOUR DATE TO HAVE THE EVENING PLANNED. BE SURE YOU CAN SUGGEST SOMETHING IF HE

DOESN'T HAVE AN IDEA OR IF YOU DON'T LIKE WHAT HE SUGGESTS.

3. BRING MONEY. JUST BECAUSE A GUY ASKS YOU OUT DOESN'T MEAN HE WILL PAY FOR YOU. AND THERE'S NOTHING WRONG WITH A GIRL PAYING FOR A DATE. IT'S GOOD TO HAVE MONEY WITH YOU ANYWAY IN CASE OF AN EMERGENCY.

Pam settled on wearing her turquoise shirt and jeans. "Now what? Makeup?"

"No, something better. But don't overdo it!" I handed her the bottle of Opium perfume that Darlene had lent me.

Pam carefully dabbed a little of the perfume on her neck and wrists. She looked at the clock. "It's almost seven thirty," she said. "Oh, I'm so glad you're here. I would die if you weren't."

I continued reading:

4. TELL YOUR PARENTS A LITTLE ABOUT YOUR DATE SO WHEN THEY MEET HIM THEY'LL HAVE SOMETHING TO TALK TO HIM ABOUT. BUT DON'T LEAVE THEM TALKING ALONE TOO LONG.

"I already told my parents everything about him," Pam confided. "I couldn't help it. I've been such a nervous wreck. I think they're tired of hearing his name."

When the doorbell rang, we waited a minute and then Pam walked out of her room. She glanced back at me.

"Have fun and call me in the morning!" I whispered.

"You too," she said. "Can you believe it? We both have dates on a Saturday night!"

"Mine's not a date," I reminded her. "Now get out of here."

When I heard the front door close, I rushed downstairs to grill her parents.

"Well, what did you think? What was he wearing? What did he say?"

Pam's mom started laughing. "He looked very handsome, and he was wearing khaki pants and a red sweater."

"And they were going to have pizza," her father informed me.

"I hear you have a little date yourself, young lady," Pam's mom said.

"It's not a date. I'm just having dinner at Spike's house."

"Oh," they both said at the same time, with that knowing look that parents are so good at giving.

"What time is your nondate?" asked Pam's mom.

"Now," I said. "I guess it's time to go." I went into the bathroom before I left and brushed my hair. I dabbed a bit of perfume under my neck. If only I were on my way to Patrick's house, I thought.

"Ciao, Marcella!" Spike greeted me with an Italian accent. He was wearing a lime-green cooking smock that said I NEVER MET A CARBOHYDRATE I DIDN'T LIKE.

"Hi, Spike." What a nut, I thought.

"I decided that we had to have pasta tonight because we're going on a bike ride tomorrow and we need our carbos."

"We are?"

"Do you already have plans?" he asked.

"Well, no."

"Then we are. Now follow me into the kitchen before the whole dinner boils over." The aroma of garlic and tomatoes filled the house. There were pots on the stove and dishes, wrappers and utensils all over the counter and in the sink.

"Here, have some sparkling apple cider." He handed me a glass. "Are you hungry?"

"Yes."

"Good, 'cause I'm starving!" He opened the refrigerator and took out a tray of marinated vegetables and sliced meats. "It's antipasto," he said, setting the tray on the table. "Then comes my famous spaghetti and salad Italiano."

"This looks wonderful," I told him. I filled my plate with a little of everything. Spike did the same.

While we ate our antipasto, Spike kept jumping up to stir the sauce, to check on the spaghetti, to put the garlic bread in the oven. He asked me if I knew when the pasta would be done.

"You can throw a strand on the ceiling," I said. "If it sticks, it's ready."

I giggled as Spike tried to reach the high ceiling with the spaghetti. It kept falling back down. Finally he announced that it was ready.

"How do you know?" I asked.

"Because when it landed on my head, it stuck. Oh no! The garlic bread!" Spike dashed for the oven. He opened the door and smoke poured into the kitchen. "You don't like garlic bread, do you?"

"Naw," I said. "I hate it."

We finally sat down to dinner. We sipped our cider, ate our spaghetti and talked about everything from the newspaper to Spike's bike race to our families to school to Pam's date. Spike asked me about Patrick, and I told him the whole story, including the fact that Patrick hadn't called me.

"He's not good enough for you then," Spike declared. "Any guy would be lucky to have you as a girlfriend." I blushed. Spike had a way of making me feel really good about myself.

Together we cleared the table and washed the dishes. Spike's dad drove me home at ten thirty.

Pam called at eight the next morning. I was still half asleep when I picked up the phone.

"Marci, my date was awesome! Tony's so nice I could die!"

"So you had fun?"

"Fun is an understatement. He's the most wonderful guy I've ever met."

I started to wake up. "Tell me everything!"

"Well, first we went to have pizza. We talked about school and volleyball and our families. Marci, you wouldn't believe it. We just talked and talked and talked."

"And then?"

"And then we went over to the arcade and played Pac-Man and pinball. We had a blast. His dad picked us up at ten."

"Aren't you leaving something out?"

"He kissed me!" she practically shouted into the phone. "Right before his dad came to pick us up, while we were standing outside the arcade. He's the best kisser in the whole world!"

"How would you know?"

"Oh, I just know," she said, sounding a bit hurt.

"So, when do you see him again?"

"We're going to the mall today," she said dreamily. "Oh, yeah," she added. "I asked him about Patrick."

"And?" I was suddenly wide awake.

"He said that he's not that good friends with Patrick but he *thought* that Patrick liked you."

"Anything else?"

"No, that's all."

"Well, I better get ready for my bike ride," I told her.

"Bike ride? With who?"

"Spike."

"Marci, I think Spike likes you more than as a friend," warned Pam.

"No, we're just pals."

"Okaaay," she said. I knew she didn't believe me. "Have fun!"

11

After school the next day Pam and I met in Coach Stratton's office. He told us that besides keeping score at the volleyball game, we had to take roll on the bus.

"Don't let the guys intimidate you," he said as we got ready to leave. "They can be obnoxious when they get together. Sit in the front of the bus with me if you want. It's only half an hour to Fox Hill Junior High."

Pam and I followed him to the bus. At least twenty guys were waiting outside it.

"Guys, listen up!" the coach called. "I'd like you to meet our new team managers, Marci and Pam."

There were hoots and howls. It was so embarrassing!

Coach Stratton glared at them. "Let's get moving," he barked. "Everyone check that you have your uniforms and take a seat."

The guys filed onto the bus. I noticed Patrick at the back of the line. He was looking in my direction. I looked the other way. When all the guys were seated, Pam and I followed the coach onto the bus.

"Hey, come sit with us!" someone called from the back.

"It's much more fun in the back!" came another voice.

I looked at Pam. She rolled her eyes. We sat down next to Coach Stratton in the front seat.

"Are you going to be good luck for us?" another guy shouted. More laughter.

"You'd be better luck if you sat back here!" someone else called.

Coach Stratton shook his head.

"What grade are you in?" another voice yelled out.

"Hey, leave them alone, would you?" we heard someone say.

"That was Tony," Pam whispered.

I turned around and tried to spot Patrick, but I couldn't.

"Tony," a guy called. "Is there something you want to tell us?"

Pam blushed.

Coach Stratton stood up. "That's enough, guys!" The team quieted down. The coach took roll and the bus moved out of the parking lot.

He leaned toward us. "I'll let you take roll another time," he said. "Once they get used to having you around."

It seemed like forever before we got to Fox Hill. When we did, everyone filed off the bus. Some carried equipment, others just walked into the gym. Pam and I followed the coach into the big cement building and sat down on a bench facing the court. The Fox Hill team was already warming up. The Franklin team was scattered around the gym. Pam walked off to talk to Tony. I sat alone, not sure what to do.

Then someone sat down next to me. It was Patrick, looking tan and muscular in his blue tank top and shorts.

"Hi," he said. "Long time no see."

Be confident, I instructed myself. "How's it going?" I asked.

"Pretty good," he said. "I'm psyched for the game."

"Well, I hope you win," I told him.

"No question about it," he said confidently. Then he looked into my eyes. "So, when did you hook up with the coach to be our manager?" I was amazed at how long Patrick's eyelashes were.

"Last week," I replied. I wondered briefly if he thought I did it because of him. "He asked me if I wanted to do it," I lied. "I figured, why not?"

"Well, good," he said, smiling. "I'll get to see more of you." I felt weak, but I managed to smile too. "Catch you later." He jogged away.

Pam came running over. "Well?" she demanded. "What did he say? Tell me!"

I told her everything.

Pam wagged her finger at me. "See? I knew he liked you."

"Maybe he does," I admitted cautiously.

Then I saw Patrick saunter up to the Franklin cheerleaders, who were huddled in a corner. He said something, and they all laughed. I looked away. Pam put her arm around me. "Don't worry," she whispered. "He's just a flirt."

"Great," I grouched. "And he probably didn't have to study flirting, either. He was probably born knowing how."

When the game started, I couldn't keep my eyes off

TDH. But then how *could* I avoid staring at him? He was the star of the game. Every once in a while after a point he would look over at me and smile. Each time he did it, I felt giddy. Then I noticed that I wasn't the only girl he was smiling at. I caught him smiling at the cheerleaders, and then at a blond girl in the stands. I tried not to watch.

When Patrick made the final smash point for Franklin's victory, I squeezed Pam's hand. I would have jumped up and cheered, but the refs insist on impartial behavior from scorekeepers.

Our team huddled together on the court and shouted a cheer. The Fox Hill team did the same. Then everyone shook hands and filed off the court. Patrick walked right over to me and put his hand on my shoulder.

"What did you think?" he asked.

I looked up at him. "It was a great game. You played really well."

"Thanks," he said, and ran off. He talked to one of the cheerleaders and then joined Tony and Pam. Should I go over to them? I wondered. Or would that look like I was chasing Patrick? I just stood there, feeling weird.

Then Pam made up my mind for me. "Hey, Marci!" she called. "Come over here."

"Do you want to go celebrate our victory at Swensen's when we get back?" Patrick asked me as I joined them.

"Sure," I said. "That sounds good."

"Okay, then," said Tony. "We'd better pack up." The boys left.

Pam leaned toward me. "Can you believe it?" she whispered.

But I was in shock and couldn't speak.

When we got back to our school, it was six thirty. I called my mom from Coach Stratton's office to ask if I could go to Swensen's. She said yes and offered to pick us up at eight. Pam called her parents too.

Tony poked his head into the office. "Ready?" he asked.

We said good-bye to Coach Stratton and left. Patrick was waiting outside. He had changed into jeans and a T-shirt.

"I'm ready for some triple-fudge-nut chocolate ice cream," he said.

"Do you love chocolate too?" I asked.

"You bet!" said Patrick.

"You make a perfect match," Pam said.

I blushed and Patrick smiled at me.

When we got to Swensen's, we each ordered a burger and ice cream. Patrick and Tony started analyzing the game, and they asked us what we thought of different plays. Then we told jokes, going around the table. My stomach hurt from laughing so much.

At seven forty-five we left. We sat on a curb out front to wait for our rides. Patrick sat next to me.

"Marci, have you seen the new Mel Gibson flick?" he asked.

"No." My heartbeat quickened, but I managed to act normal.

"Me neither," he said. "Do you want to go see it Saturday?"

I couldn't believe it. "Sure."

"Okay," said Patrick. "I'll see if my brother can drive us. Why don't I give you a call later tonight?"

"Great."

A horn beeped and my mom pulled up. I smiled at Patrick, and then Pam and I got in the car.

"Well, you two sure look like you're in a good mood," my mom said. "Who were those handsome boys?"

"Our boyfriends," Pam gushed.

"Or they *will* be by Valentine's Day," I added.

Spike and Tony sat with Pam and me the next day at lunch. Patrick hadn't called, and I was dying to ask Tony if he knew what was going on. But I was too embarrassed.

"We need to collect the questionnaires and start working on the final article," Spike began. I nudged him, hoping he'd be quiet. I was sure Pam wouldn't want Tony to know we had written the questionnaire. She saw me.

"Oh, don't worry," she said. "I told Tony all about it."

I was shocked. And a little hurt, too. Why hadn't Pam told me that she'd told him?

"So," Spike continued, "how about picking up the forms at lunch Friday so we can work on the article that night? I'd like to have it finished by next week."

"Fine by me," I said.

"Me too," put in Pam. She glanced at Tony. "Would it be all right if Tony helped?"

"Sure," I told her. What did she expect us to say with him sitting there?

"The more the merrier," said Spike.

I went straight home after school that day so I wouldn't miss Patrick if he called. Spike had asked if I wanted to go for a bike ride, but I'd said no.

When Darlene got home, I was sitting in the living room with my science homework spread out in front of me. I had doodled a giant heart on the top of my assignment paper and filled it with ten little ones.

"No phone call?" she asked. I shook my head.

"Marci, maybe it would be better if you weren't home when he calls. You don't want him to think you're sitting by the phone."

"I have homework to do," I said. "I'm not just sitting by the phone."

Darlene shrugged. "Okay," she said. "But I think you should forget about Patrick. If he's unreliable in the beginning, he can only get worse. Why not go for Spike? He really likes you, and I think he's adorable!"

I shook my head. I knew Spike liked me, but I couldn't get my mind off Patrick. For some reason, it just wasn't the same with Spike.

Darlene shrugged again and went upstairs. The phone rang.

"Marci, phone!" she called.

I picked it up. "Hello?"

"Hi, Marci, this is Patrick."

"Hi," I squeaked.

"Um . . . I just called to see if you still wanted to go to the movie Saturday. My brother Mark said he could drive us."

"Great," I said.

"So, why don't we pick you up at nine. The movie starts at nine fifteen."

"Well," I said, "I can only go to the early show. You know mothers."

"Oh," said Patrick. "Hold on and I'll talk to Mark."

I felt really stupid. I had argued with my mother about going to the later show, but she had insisted that I was too young. "I don't know Patrick," she had said. "So unless I speak to his parents, you can only go to the early show." I was too embarrassed to have her call Patrick's house.

"Mark said that's fine," Patrick informed me when he came back on. "How about six thirty?"

"That's perfect." I told him where I lived.

"I'll see you at school."

"Right," I said. "Bye."

I sat there, silent and dazed. Darlene ran down the stairs.

"You have a date!" she yelled.

I did. And it was with Patrick Bell—*the* Patrick Bell. He could go out with *any* girl in school—and he had asked me!

The rest of the week flew by. Before I knew it, it was Friday afternoon and Pam, Tony and Spike were settling down in my living room to work on our article.

When everyone was comfortable, we each took a stack of questionnaires. We read through them fairly quickly the first time, separating the more interesting answers from the rest.

For instance, most of the kids rated their personal traits and popularity from 5 to 8. That meant that the majority of kids thought they were a little better than average. It was the low and high answers that we set apart. We did the same for "How good a friend are you?" Almost all the kids thought they were extremely reliable, thoughtful, loyal, honest and good listeners.

Some of the responses really surprised me. Most of the kids wrote that they were just as comfortable talking to friends of the opposite sex as they were talking to crushes. That certainly wasn't true for me. I was much more nervous talking to Patrick than I was talking to Spike. I wondered how honest the kids had been.

Almost everybody wrote that they'd been on dates, mostly to the mall, the movies, parties or friends' houses. But one fourteen-year-old girl wanted to go to "an elegant café to have a cozy, candle-lit dinner."

"She's got class," declared Pam.

"And I've found her a date," said Spike. "Here's a fourteen-year-old guy who also wants to have a candle-lit dinner."

"If we knew who they were, we could set them up," I joked. We laughed.

Responses to what makes someone a boyfriend or girlfriend varied from sarcastic sexual remarks to honest explanations. Our favorite was written by a seventh-grade girl.

"A boyfriend is someone who cares about you, who doesn't use you and who likes you for who you are," she wrote. We thought that was very mature.

Of the girls who *did* have boyfriends, a lot complained that the guys took up too much of their time and that they missed being with their female friends. One girl wrote, "I've had it with George! If he wants to be my boyfriend, he better stop making fun of Paula.

She's my best friend, and I'm not going to sit back and watch her get hurt. She's worth more to me than any guy."

Some of the boys with girlfriends commented that the girls demanded too much time. "Carole wants me to stop playing football to spend more time with her," wrote one guy. "Sorry, babe—it's not going to happen!" Another boy complained that his girlfriend "throws a fit if I don't call her every day."

Of the kids without partners, a lot of insecurities were expressed. "I feel like there's something missing in my life," an eighth-grade girl wrote. "I know that a boyfriend would solve all my problems."

Spike turned to me. "Do you feel that way?"

"No," I replied uncomfortably. I sort of did, but I didn't want to admit it.

Most of the kids wrote that they'd never been in love. "I've never been in love and I don't think I ever will be," wrote a seventh-grade girl. "When I like a guy, I'm too nervous to talk to him."

Some answers made us really sad. "I feel like a reject, a castoff," a girl wrote. "How could I know what it's like to be in love when no one will even talk to me?" Pam, Tony, Spike and I wished that we could help her somehow. What a horrible way to feel!

"I want so badly to be in love," wrote an eighth-grade girl. "Now that my friends have boyfriends, they never call me anymore."

Another girl wrote, "I've been in love since the first time I saw Tim in English class—four months and three days ago. I think about him twenty-four hours a day. The problem is that he's adorable and popular. I'm ugly, and I've got no friends. I know he could never love me back." Reading answers like these made me realize my problems weren't so bad.

Some of the boys were also open about their feelings. A seventh-grade guy wrote that he was most self-conscious when he went out with a girl. And another boy was worried about "looking like a spaz" when he went on a date.

"They think just like we do," Pam said in awe. "And they're *boys*!"

"Oooh! Not *boys*!" teased Spike. Pam pushed him.

"But listen to this," I put in. "Here's a more typical *boy* answer. For what makes someone a girlfriend an eighth-grade guy wrote, 'Sex on a regular basis.' And for where he'd most like to go on a date he wrote, 'To a cheap motel.'"

"Seee?" drawled Pam.

When we tallied up the answers to "What would you look for in a boyfriend/girlfriend?" we saw that the boys answered a lot differently from the girls. The categories rated highest by the girls were "honesty," "sense of humor," "reliability," "looks."

A few of the boys agreed with those answers, but most rated *every* category with a ten and a lot wrote obnoxious comments like "big boobs" or "good in bed" in the space next to "other."

"Do guys really think that way?" Pam asked.

"Only when they're being jerks," declared Spike.

"What do you guys look for in a girlfriend?" I asked.

Tony blushed and said, "Pam."

Spike said he wanted someone who was reliable, intelligent, had a sense of humor and was friendly. "And of course, good looking wouldn't hurt," he added.

We sat up until nine reading over the answers. We

concluded that everyone was insecure, even the guys who wrote dumb answers.

"They're probably the most insecure," commented Spike.

Darlene helped us organize our information and come up with an outline for the article. She suggested that we use some of the information from the books we read and back that up with statistics and quotes from the questionnaires. She helped us pick which answers to quote from and which to paraphrase. It was fascinating to put the whole thing together.

By eleven we were exhausted. We knew *how* we were going to write the story, but now we had to actually write it. Spike, Pam and I agreed that we would work on it during the week. Mr. Thompson was counting on the article for the next issue.

13

"Oh, Pam, I don't know what to wear!" I wailed. I had tried on everything in my closet, plus the clothes Pam had brought over. My room looked like a picked-over garage sale!

I stood in front of the mirror in my black jeans and a purple sweater. All I could see was the enormous pimple that had decided today was its day to appear— right in the middle of my forehead.

"Ugh!" I said.

"Marci, you can't even see it," Pam said. "You're just paranoid."

"What do you mean, you can't see it? It's huge!"

Pam laughed. "Stop it. You look fine! Now take off that sweater and try on this one." She handed me a pink cardigan.

"No. Too preppy."

"Okay, then this one." She held up a green V-neck sweater. I put it on. "I love it!" Pam said.

"I look fat!" I announced. "Maybe I should wear a

skirt instead of pants. What if Patrick likes skirts? Do you think he likes green? What would a cheerleader wear?"

"He didn't ask a *cheerleader* out!" Darlene said as she walked into the room. "He asked *you*."

"That's right," Pam put in. "Remember what the books said—you shouldn't change for a guy. Just be yourself."

"Anything else?"

"Shut up and come here," ordered Darlene.

I obeyed. She dabbed some perfume on my neck. "Now flip your hair over," she said. I did and she sprayed a bit of hairspray on the underneath part.

"Yuck!" I coughed. I flipped my hair back and Darlene teased it with the brush.

"Beautiful!"

"Now what?" I asked.

"Now you wait," advised Pam. "It's six thirty-five. He's late."

Then the doorbell rang. We all looked at each other.

"I'll get it!" Timmy yelled, charging down the stairs. Darlene followed him. I took one final look at myself in the mirror.

"Good luck," Pam said. "Call me first thing in the morning."

"Thanks," I told her.

"Marci's upstairs with Pammy," I heard Timmy say. I covered my face with my hands.

"Timmy, why don't you go get me a glass of orange juice," Darlene suggested.

"Marci's got a date!" Timmy sang on his way to the kitchen. How embarrassing!

I walked downstairs. Darlene and my mom were sitting in the living room with Patrick. He was wearing blue jeans and a blue-and-white-striped button down. He looked great.

"Hi," I said. He stood up, smiling at me.

"Well, you two better get going or you'll miss the movie," Darlene said. Thank God for sisters.

"Right," agreed Patrick.

"Bye," I said.

"Have fun!" called my mom.

We walked out the door and I looked at Patrick. "I hate that meeting parents stuff," he said, and laughed.

"Me too." I smiled.

"Come on, guys!" Patrick's brother called from the car. We walked over and got into the backseat. Patrick introduced me to Mark and his girlfriend, Tania. Mark looked just like Patrick, only he was about seventeen and his hair was longer.

"Are you coming to the movie with us?" I asked.

"My parents think so." He snickered. "But we're really going to a party." Tania giggled. "Why don't you come with us?" invited Mark. "It's going to be a good one. They've got the barbecue going and there's a keg."

I looked at Patrick. I didn't want to go to a party—especially not one with high school kids . . . and a keg of beer!

"Thanks anyway," he said. "But we're really psyched to see this flick."

I was very relieved. Mark dropped us off at the theater and said he'd pick us up after the movie. People were already waiting to get in. Patrick paid for our tickets, and then we walked to the end of the line.

"Marci!" I heard someone call. It was Leslie, hanging on Peter's arm. She waved us over and I made the introductions. Leslie stared at Patrick and then back at me. Suddenly she didn't look smug at all. She looked jealous! I loved it.

"So, when did you two start going out?" she asked. Talk about blunt! But Patrick was cool.

"Oh, we've been dating for years," he said. "Didn't Marci ever tell you?" I smiled.

"Right, years," I echoed. Years? "Come on. Let's get in line." I didn't want Leslie to ask any more questions.

Before we got to the end of the line, we ran into two guys from the volleyball team. We joined them, and the guys immediately started talking about volleyball. I was beginning to wonder if they knew how to talk about anything else. Patrick was ignoring me, so I was glad when the line started moving.

We went directly to the popcorn stand and bought a medium popcorn, some M&Ms and two Cokes. I was too embarrassed to ask for a Diet Coke—after all, I didn't want him to think I thought I was fat!

"This should be a good movie," I told him as we found seats.

"Yeah," said Patrick. The lights went out. I slouched down in my seat to get more comfortable. So did Patrick. I looked over at him at the same time that he looked at me. I quickly looked away. A few minutes later the previews started. I was glad—now we didn't have to scramble for things to talk about.

Patrick took some popcorn from the box on my lap. His arm brushed against mine, and I felt shivers all the way up my arm. I relaxed a bit by the time the movie started, and after about an hour I was even feeling comfortable, although I was aware of Patrick's every move.

On the screen Mel Gibson was walking along a dark path with a woman. He stopped under a tree and kissed her. Suddenly I felt Patrick's arm on my shoulders. I stiffened and stared at the screen. What do I do now? I thought as Patrick began rubbing my arm. Meanwhile, Mel Gibson was still kissing the woman. Patrick must have gotten the message that I didn't want him to go any further, but his arm remained around my shoulders through the rest of the movie. Sexy movies should not be seen on a first date. I'd have to remember to add that to our book.

When the show was over, Patrick and I went next door to get something to drink and wait for Mark, who was supposed to be picking us up there. I ordered a large lemonade. Patrick ordered a Coke. That's when we started talking. We talked about the movie, school and our parents. He was so much nicer when he was away from his volleyball pals.

I asked Patrick how he got along with his brother, and he sighed and looked away.

"All right, I guess," he finally said. "We're just real different."

"What do you mean?" I asked.

"Oh, I don't know. All he ever thinks about is where the next party is. And he always wants me to go with him."

"Don't you like parties?"

"Yeah. But not all the time. How about you and your sister? Do you get along?"

"Well, we didn't used to," I admitted. "But I think things are changing. Last week we really talked for the first time since my parents' split."

"My brother and I have never really talked about our parents' divorce, and it's been two years. It was pretty painful for me, and I'm sure it was for him too. But neither of us ever admitted it." He paused. "Marci, I can't believe I'm telling you these things. I mean, it's just not the kind of conversation I usually have with a girl."

"You don't have to talk about it if you don't want to," I told him.

"No. I like it. I usually have trouble talking about my feelings, but with you I don't."

Just then Mark showed up. Patrick stiffened.

"How's the party?" he asked Mark.

"Great! You should come back with us."

"Maybe next time," said Patrick. "Marci has to get home." He glanced at me and smiled. "Right?"

"Right," I agreed, and smiled back.

When we arrived at my house, Patrick got out of the car and walked me to the door. I didn't know what to expect or what I should do, but Patrick took matters into his own hands. He leaned over and kissed me—a quick kiss. His lips were soft. I closed my eyes, and my whole body tingled. He kissed me again, this time longer. Then he looked at me.

"I had a really nice time tonight," he said.

"I did too. Thanks."

"So, do you want to go out again sometime?"

"Sure." I could hear the blood pounding in my ears.

"I'll see you on Monday."

"Yeah," I squeaked. "Bye." I opened the door and waved from the doorway. Patrick waved back.

I closed the door and leaned back against it. He was definitely the best kisser in the whole world!

14

I walked into my room after school on Friday and did a belly flop onto my bed. It felt as though I hadn't relaxed in years. Actually it had been only six days since my big date with Patrick, but since then I'd worked on the newspaper article every day with Spike. We'd finished it last night. Pam had helped a little, but she was too wrapped up in Tony to do much.

And on top of the newspaper work there had been a home volleyball game. Pam and I had gone out for pizza after the game with Patrick and Tony.

I still couldn't believe that I was with Patrick. He was so cute! Girls were always giving him the eye when we were together. But I was uneasy about him. One minute he'd be attentive, and the next minute he hardly knew I was there. He'd called me once this week, but two other times he told me he'd call and then he didn't. When we did talk, our conversations tended to be short and they usually focused on his favorite topic—volleyball.

Why couldn't we talk the way we did on our first

date? I wondered. That was the Patrick that I liked and I felt comfortable with. This other Patrick was too concerned with his image. Maybe it was my fault. I could never be myself around him when he acted that way.

Was this what having a boyfriend was supposed to be like? I wasn't sure how I felt about it. Maybe I wasn't ready to have a boyfriend. Pam didn't have problems like this with Tony, so I knew she was ready. I wasn't even sure if I could call Patrick my boyfriend. He told me he liked me, but he didn't do much to show it. He hadn't even asked me to the Valentine's Day dance, and it was only eight days away. Tony had asked Pam long ago, and she was already trying to decide what to wear.

I sat up and reached for our secret book. I flipped to the page where Pam and I had written down what we wanted in a boyfriend.

1. CUTE
2. ATHLETIC
3. POPULAR
4. FUNNY
5. NICE

I picked up a pen. Next to the list I wrote:

1. RELIABLE
2. THOUGHTFUL
3. SENSE OF HUMOR
4. HONEST
5. GOOD LISTENER
6. FRIENDLY (ALL THE TIME)

I leaned back and laid the open book on my stomach. This second list was more like it. Maybe the books we read were right. Cute wasn't everything. In fact, it just seemed to cause problems. True, it was fun being seen with Patrick. I loved the way he looked. But here I was, alone on a Friday night with no plans for the weekend. Darlene was going out with Bill, and Pam was going out with Tony.

I heard the phone ring. It was Spike. We talked about the article, school, our puppies, everything. Talking to Spike was practically like talking to Pam. But suddenly he ran out of things to say and there was an uncomfortable silence.

"Spike, is something wrong?" I asked.

"No. I just, well, I wanted to ask you something."

"So, ask away," I told him.

"Well, do you want to go to the Valentine's Day dance with me? Of course, it would have to be an early night because I have to get up for my race the next morning."

I groaned silently and thought about Patrick. What if he never asked me? But what if he did?

So I lied. "Spike, I'm going with Patrick."

"Oh."

"I'm sorry."

"Hey, no problem."

"Yeah." I let out a breath.

"Okay," he said. "Well, see ya."

Pam called me at nine thirty the next morning. "I asked Tony if Patrick said anything about taking you to the dance," she said. "But he said they hadn't talked about the dance at all."

"Oh." I sighed. "Spike asked me to go."

"He did? What did you say?"

"That I was going with Patrick. Oh, Pam, what am I going to do?"

"Well, Tony and I think Patrick will ask you. I mean, it *seems* like you two are a couple."

"But it's only seven days away."

Pam didn't say anything.

"I guess I'm not going to make our pact." I took a deep breath to keep from crying.

"Oh, Marci, don't worry. It was a dumb idea anyway. It's not important."

"Sure. Because *you* have a boyfriend."

"Don't be mad at me," Pam begged. "I was just lucky with Tony. You'll meet someone too."

"I'm not mad." I sighed. "I'm sorry. I'm just depressed."

"What you need is some cheering up! Do you want to come over and watch TV with us tonight? We have chocolate ice cream!"

Right, I thought. Just what I'd like to do. Sit there while you and Tony make eyes at each other. "Thanks anyway," I told her.

"Okay. How about coming shopping with me today?"

"Sure," I said. "Why not?"

"Great. I'll come by in a little while."

"Bye."

When Pam and I got to the mall, we went straight to the card shop. Pam wanted to pick out a Valentine's Day card for Tony. I thought maybe I'd buy Patrick one too, but every card talked about love. The store was crowded. Everyone has someone to buy a Valentine's Day card for but me, I thought. My eyes filled with tears. Pam picked out one that had a picture of a woman doing a backward flip on the cover. It said, "I've flipped over you."

I found a card that had a picture of a cat struggling up a flight of stairs, with one paw on the top step. The inside read, "It's a hard climb to the top. Good luck." I bought it to give to Spike before his big bike race next week.

Spike called at three, just when I got home. He wanted to go for a bike ride. I took his mountain bike and he took Primo. We rode past school and down to the beach.

"I'll race you to the lemonade stand," Spike announced. "Last one there buys." He took off. I, of course, paid for the drinks.

By the time I got home I was exhausted, but I also felt a lot better. Spike had recited Monty Python scenes the whole way home. I had laughed so hard I almost fell off my bike.

The phone rang. I picked it up.

"Spam, Spam, Spam, Spam," Spike sang into the phone with a British accent.

"Spike, you are too weird."

He laughed. "Just checking to see if you made it home," he said. "Bye."

"Bye." I hung up, shaking my head. He was such a nut.

Before I got out of the living room, the phone rang again. I picked it right up. It had to be Spike again.

"Spam, Spam, Spam, Spam," I sang into the receiver.

"Uh . . . is . . . is Marci there?" a male voice stammered. Oh, God! It was Patrick.

I disguised my voice, making it deeper. "Just a minute," I said. I covered the phone for a minute. Then I took a deep breath and uncovered it.

"Hello," I said.

"Hi, Marci. This is Patrick."

"Oh, hi. How are you?"

"Pretty good. I just got finished playing volleyball, and I'm beat. Listen, I called to see if you wanted to go to the beach tomorrow. It's supposed to be seventy-five degrees. Can you believe this weather in the middle of February?"

"It's fantastic," I said. "And I'd love to go to the beach."

"Okay. I'll call you in the morning."

"Great!"

"Bye," he said.

"Bye." I hung up and lay back on the couch.

This was it! He was bound to ask me to the dance tomorrow.

16

The next morning I woke up at seven thirty. I tried on three bathing suits and five pairs of shorts before deciding on the right beach outfit for the day—a pink one-piece, denim shorts and a white shirt. A headline on the front page of the *LA Times* said WINTER WARMS UP, and the paper predicted a high of eighty degrees.

I went downstairs and drank a glass of orange juice. I didn't dare eat anything since I'd be in a bathing suit all day. Then I sat in the living room with Timmy and Ninja. We played a game of War, and I let Timmy win. When the game was over, he picked up the cards and threw them all over the floor.

"Fifty-two card pickup!" Timmy yelled, and fell back laughing. Ninja ran around barking and sliding over the cards.

I shook my head. "You spaz! Now help me pick up every one of those fifty-two cards."

My mom walked in. "What time are you going to the beach?"

"I don't know," I told her. "I'm still waiting to hear."

Darlene was sure he wouldn't call before ten. Pam predicted an eleven o'clock phone call. I figured ten thirty.

At nine the phone rang. He's early, I thought, and picked up the phone.

"Hi, Marci." It was my father.

"Hi, Dad."

"What are you doing today? I thought I'd come up and maybe we could do something together."

"Sorry, Dad," I said. "I have a date."

"A date? Who do you have a date with?"

I told him all about Patrick. Darlene walked into the room.

"Wow," he marveled. "You sure are growing up!" I laughed. "How about Darlene? What's she doing today?"

I put my hand over the receiver and whispered to Darlene that it was Dad. She nodded.

"Hang on," I told him. I handed her the phone.

"Sorry, Dad," she said. "I've got plans with Bill." They talked for a few more minutes, and then she passed the phone over to Timmy.

"What are you doing with Bill today?" I asked Darlene.

"Oh, I don't have any plans," she admitted. "I'm just not ready to see Dad yet."

The phone didn't ring again until eleven thirty. My hand was shaking when I answered it.

"Hi, Marci," said Pam. "Has he called yet?"

"No."

"Oh. Well, I'm sure he just slept late," she said. "He'll call soon."

"Right."

"Call me when he does."

"Okay." We hung up.

I turned on the TV. There was an old Gidget movie on, with girls running along the beach in funny-looking bathing suits and big puffy hairstyles.

I turned off the TV at one. Patrick still hadn't called.

By two I had decided that I hated boys. Then the phone rang. It was Pam.

"Still no call?"

"No."

"I think he's a jerk, Marci. How could he ask you out and then stand you up?"

"I don't know. Maybe he forgot." My eyes filled with tears.

"Well, then you shouldn't go out with him if he thinks you're forgettable. He's stupid." I didn't say anything because I was sure I would start crying if I opened my mouth. "Come to the beach with Tony and me," offered Pam. "We're going right now."

"No, thanks," I managed to say. "I'm not in a beach mood anymore."

"Okay," Pam said. "But don't be depressed. You're too good for Patrick anyway." We hung up.

At three Darlene said that she wouldn't let me go to the beach with Patrick even if he did call.

"In fact," she said, throwing her head back, "I don't think you should ever speak to him again. I'd like to call him right now and tell him what I think of him. No one treats my sister like this."

I looked away. I didn't want Darlene to know how upset I was. "It's all right," I finally said. "I'm sure Patrick has a good explanation. It's not a big deal. Really."

Darlene shook her head. I knew I hadn't fooled her. She answered the phone each time it rang, saying she'd tell Patrick I wasn't home.

She didn't have to.

The next day at school I looked for Patrick, but I didn't see him. I had promised Coach Stratton that I would take roll at practice after school. He had to be in a meeting until three thirty and wanted to make sure the team was on time—three fifteen sharp. Pam came with me.

Patrick strutted into the gym at three thirty. He waved at me, but I pretended not to notice. Then I marked him late on the roll sheet—it served him right! He joined the guys, who were taking turns spiking the ball over the net. Pam and I were sitting at one end of the middle court, yelling out names. I still didn't know who half the guys were.

"Ahhh!" Pam screamed as a ball flew by an inch from her nose. Another ball skimmed our heads. We ducked, laughing.

"I better write my will," I said. "I leave all my clothes to you, my room to Darlene and all my photos of myself to my parents."

Pam laughed again. "And I leave everything to you. My parents wouldn't want my junk." We carried our chairs over to the side court as balls flew everywhere. Just as we sat down again Patrick jumped high in the air and spiked the ball over the net. It shot straight at us. I covered my head with my hands.

He came running over. "Sorry about that," he apologized. But he kept running, picked up the ball and ran back in line. Pam looked at me. I took a deep breath and looked away.

Fifteen minutes later, we were finished taking roll. I wanted to go home, but we still had to wait for Coach Stratton. Pam left to talk to Tony. I stared at the roll book.

"Hey," a voice said. Patrick was standing over me.

"Hi." I refused to look up, pretending I was very busy.

"Listen, I'm sorry about yesterday. Mark wanted me to go with him to buy a stereo, and I never made it to the beach."

You could have called, I thought. "Oh," was all I said.

"We'll go another time!" He touched my shoulder and smiled. "Okay?"

Why is he so incredibly cute? I thought. I sort of smiled back but didn't say anything. He darted back in line.

"Some excuse," Pam remarked when I told her. "I don't think you should waste your time on Patrick. You're only going to get hurt."

I knew Pam was right. And so was Darlene. I hated the way Patrick was treating me. It made me feel awful. But I also knew how wonderful I felt when we were alone. His split personality was sending me on a roller-coaster ride. I was so confused.

Coach Stratton returned just then, so Pam and I made a quick exit.

On my way to gym class the next day someone grabbed me from behind and twirled me around. There I was, practically nose to nose with Patrick.

"Hey, beautiful," he said. "What time should I pick you up for the dance?"

I was so stunned that I could hardly speak. "I don't know," I squeaked.

"How about eight?"

"Sure."

"See you then," he said. "I've got to get to class." He flashed me a big smile and took off.

Pam got to my house at five Saturday night. Even though we weren't going to the dance in the same car, we'd decided to get dressed together. Tony was going to pick her up at my house—his mom was driving. Mark was taking Patrick and me to the dance, and Darlene was picking us up.

Pam and Darlene had been furious when I told them I was going to the dance with Patrick.

"How do you know he'll show up?" Darlene had said.

"Because I trust him," I'd lied. Then I told them that if he was a jerk at the dance, I'd dump him, so they backed off a bit.

And now that it was two hours before the dance, we were all too excited to worry about it.

"Can you believe we both have boyfriends?" Pam exclaimed, readjusting her belt for the fifth time. "We kept our pact!"

I smiled. I still didn't think I could call Patrick my

boyfriend, but Pam had assured me I could. She said that if he asked me to the dance, he must be my boyfriend. I certainly wanted it to be true.

Darlene had clipped my hair up in several sections and was curling it one section at a time. The doorbell rang.

Pam grabbed my arm. "Oh, my God. What if they're early?"

"An hour and a half early?" Darlene laughed. "I doubt it."

"Girls, there's something here for you," my mother called.

The three of us stampeded downstairs. A flower arrangement—pink and white roses—sat on our coffee table. The envelope was addressed, "To Darlene and Marci."

Darlene ripped it open and read, "'To my two favorite women. Happy Valentine's Day. I love you.'" She hesitated and then finished, "'Dad.'"

"That's so sweet!" Pam cried. "Your dad is so nice."

"I'll call and thank him," I volunteered.

"No," Darlene said. "I'll do it. I think I'd like to try to get together with him anyway. It's about time we talked in person."

I hugged her. So did my mom.

"Oh, get out of here." Darlene smiled and wiped her eyes. "You're making me cry." Pam and I walked upstairs as Darlene picked up the phone.

By the time seven forty-five rolled around, I was a wreck. So was Pam. And so was Darlene—she said we were making her nervous with all our fussing.

"You're doing most of the fussing," I pointed out. She was curling my hair for the fourth time.

The phone rang, and my mom called that it was for me. I hesitated before picking up the phone. I had this feeling it would be Patrick, canceling.

"Hey, Marci," Spike said. "Thanks for the card."

"You're welcome." I had left the card on his door-step that afternoon. "Good luck tomorrow!" I told him. "We'll go celebrate your victory tomorrow night."

"It's a deal," he agreed. "Are you excited about the dance?"

"Sure," I said. I felt bad. I knew that Spike really liked me and I had rejected him in favor of Patrick. It must have been hard for him to call. "Are you going?" I asked.

"Naw, I've got to be up early for the race. Maybe I'll stop by for a minute, but that's it."

"Well, good luck tomorrow," I said again.

"Thanks. Bye."

It was weird to feel uncomfortable talking to Spike— I didn't like it. I hoped things between us would feel more normal after the dance.

Just as I walked back into my room the doorbell rang. Pam and I squealed. Patrick and Tony had arrived.

Darlene brushed my hair back one last time. I was wearing one of her dresses—a red one with a scoop neck and a low-cut back. She said I looked sexy in it.

"Have fun," Darlene told us.

"Thanks," Pam and I said in unison. We went down-stairs.

My mother and Timmy were in the living room with the two guys. Patrick was wearing gray pants and a salmon-colored sweater. He looked gorgeous. I took a deep breath and smiled at him. He smiled back. Pam and Tony left first. We were right behind them.

As Patrick and I walked outside he said, "You look beautiful."

"Thanks." I blushed. "You look great too."

A Talking Heads song was blaring on the radio as we got in the car. Mark was tapping the steering wheel, and Tania was singing along. Patrick and I sat silently in the back. Who could talk over that loud music?

When we got to the school, I got out of the car quickly. Patrick said something to Mark, and then we went into the gym.

It was hard to believe that this was the same place where I sweated every day. There were red and pink streamers flowing from the ceiling and rafters and big red paper hearts hanging from strings. A band was playing on a small stage with a canopy over it. There were about ten couples dancing, but crowds of kids hugged the walls.

"Let's go over and talk to Pam and Tony," I suggested when I saw them by the refreshment stand.

"Go ahead. I'll be over in a minute."

Pam and Tony were drinking punch. I helped myself to a glass of orange juice and a cookie.

"Can you believe how beautiful everyone looks?" Pam said to me.

I shook my head. "It's hard to recognize them." I scanned the room until I spotted Patrick, and my heart stopped. He was standing in the corner talking to three girls! As the band played "Twist and Shout," I looked away.

"I love this song," Pam was saying. "Let's dance."

"Let's go," Tony said.

Then Pam stopped. "Oh. I'm sorry, Marci. Go grab Patrick and come dance."

"No, thanks. I don't feel like dancing right now."

"Come with us, without Patrick," she urged. She'd spotted him too.

"No, really. I'm not in the mood."

"Okaaay," she said. "See you soon." Then she moved onto the dance floor.

I stood there with my juice in hand, alone. Patrick had now moved to a larger group of girls and guys. I looked around the room. Practically everyone I knew was on the dance floor. Leslie and Peter danced by. Leslie waved. I forced myself to smile and wave back. But I felt horrible. Three songs later Pam and Tony rejoined me.

"Why is he being such a jerk?" I asked Pam while Tony was off getting drink refills.

"I don't know what his problem is," Pam told me. "But I don't understand why you put up with it."

"I don't either," I confided. Then Tony returned. While Pam and Tony talked, I went over in my mind what I wanted to say to Patrick.

"Just because you're popular doesn't mean you can treat me like this," I could say. Or, "If you plan to take me out, you'll have to change."

A few minutes later Patrick came over.

"Let's dance," he said.

"Sure." I followed him onto the dance floor without saying a word. The band played "Roll With It." I wondered if I was dancing all right. Patrick moved easily to the music. The next song was "Straight Up," and then the band stopped for a ten-minute break. I followed

Patrick to where two guys from the volleyball team were standing. Then he introduced me to three girls. One of the girls smiled flirtatiously at Patrick, and he smiled back! I tried not to notice. How *could* he flirt with other girls right in front of me? I fumed.

When the band came back, Patrick and I danced again. Pam and Tony joined us on the dance floor. Pam and I kept switching places and spinning around. It was a lot of fun. At the end of the third song Patrick grabbed my hand.

"Come outside for a minute," he said. "I'm boiling."

I felt goose bumps on my arm when he touched me. We walked outside, holding hands. I didn't understand what I was feeling. One moment I hated Patrick and the next moment I just wanted to be close to him. Patrick led me to the front of the school, and we sat down on the edge of a planter.

"Let's get out of here," he said. I looked at my watch. It was only nine thirty.

"Where to?"

"I asked Mark to swing by about now. He's going to a great beach party at Station 18." That was where all the really wild parties went on. Darlene had told me about them. She said she hated that scene because there was too much drinking.

"I'm having fun here," I protested. "Why don't we just stay?"

"Oh, come on, Marci," Patrick said. He put his hands on my shoulders and looked into my eyes. "Be adventurous."

"What if we aren't back by ten thirty, when Darlene's picking us up?" I asked. "Besides, I thought you didn't like parties."

"We'll be back," he reasoned. "And sometimes I *do* like parties." He leaned over and kissed me lightly on the lips. "It'll be fun. Don't you trust me?"

"Well, yes," I said hesitantly. But I wasn't sure I did. And I knew for sure that I didn't trust Mark.

"Then what's the problem? Really, you'll have fun."

"Okay." I felt stupid saying anything else. "But I have to tell Pam I'm going."

"Sure," he agreed. "I'll wait here."

I went inside and told Pam and Tony about the beach party.

"No way!" Pam exclaimed. "Marci, you know about those parties. The kids are in high school. And they're all into drinking and drugs."

"Just stay here with us," invited Tony. "Let Patrick go if he wants to." Was it my imagination or was Tony getting critical of Patrick?

I didn't really know what to do. Except that I didn't want to lose Patrick.

"I'm going," I told them.

Pam stared at me. I knew she was angry. I looked at my shoes.

"Fine," she huffed.

"I'll be okay," I said.

Her look turned concerned. "Be careful," she said, touching my shoulder.

"I will." I walked away and didn't look back.

18

When I got outside, Mark and Tania were already there. Patrick was talking to them through the car window. As we climbed into the backseat Mark handed Patrick a beer.

"Do you want one, Marci?" he asked.

"No," I replied. I didn't like this at all!

Patrick opened the can and took a sip. I sat stonily as we drove. I wanted to say, "Turn around! Take me back." But I was too embarrassed.

It took us ten minutes to get to the beach. Tons of cars were parked along the side of the road, and I could hear music playing. There must have been at least a hundred kids milling around on the beach. My stomach lurched and my heart was pounding. I followed Patrick down a dirt path to get to the sand. He walked casually through the crowd and then stopped to talk to three guys. He introduced me and told me they were on the high school volleyball team.

When we continued through the crowd, Patrick stopped every few minutes to say hello to someone else. I spotted two guys from the Franklin volleyball team and waved at them. When I turned back, Patrick was gone. I looked around frantically, then I started to walk, bumping into bodies with unfamiliar faces. I didn't see Patrick anywhere. Or Mark and Tania.

"Hey, what's going on?" A blond-haired guy I'd never seen before pushed his face into mine. I could smell alcohol on his breath, and he was swaying back and forth. I kept walking. He moved with me. "What's your name?" he asked, and belched.

"M-Marci," I stuttered, and stepped back.

A girl tapped me on the shoulder. She was bouncing to the blaring sound of "Desire," by U2. "You want a beer?" she asked. She was standing next to the keg. She held out a cup so full that beer sloshed over the sides. My head was throbbing. I stumbled on.

"Hi," said a short, stocky guy blocking my way. I tried to smile, backing up quickly. He followed. I moved farther away. Then I tripped on a piece of driftwood and stumbled backward. Someone caught me.

"Be careful," warned a tall guy. "Aren't you too young to be here?" Tears filled my eyes. I pushed him away and ran through the crowd. I hate Patrick, I thought as I fought my way through the bodies.

Finally I managed to get away from everyone. I climbed up the dirt hill to the street and sat down on a rock. I buried my face in my hands. Tears were streaming down my cheeks. I looked at my watch. It was ten fifteen. I peered into the crowd, looking for Patrick, but everything was a blur. Suddenly someone touched my shoulder. I screamed and tried to scramble to my feet.

"Marci! It's only me, Spike." I looked up and started

crying again. Spike knelt and put his arms around me. "Hey, are you okay?"

I couldn't speak. I'd never been so glad to see someone in my life. I rested my head on Spike's shoulder, and he rubbed my back.

"It's all right," he said softly. Abruptly, his tone changed. "Where's Patrick?" he asked.

"I don't know," I said, sniffling. I dug a tissue out of my bag and blew my nose. "Wh-what are you doing here?" I asked. "I mean, how come you're not at home?"

"I stopped by the dance for a few minutes and Pam told me where you'd gone. And that you were with Mark and Patrick. I was worried. I know what these parties can be like." Spike sat down next to me and took my hand.

I leaned against him. "I'm so glad you're here. But what about your race? You need your rest."

"I'll be fine," he assured me. "You're more important to me than a race." I was overwhelmed. Then I felt wonderful. I gazed into Spike's eyes. They glittered in the moonlight. I smiled. So did he. I put my arm around his waist.

"Thanks," I said. "You know, any girl would be lucky to have you as a boyfriend."

Spike put his arms around my neck. "What about you?" he asked. "Would you want me as a boyfriend?"

I nodded. "I would love it." Spike pulled me close to him and gave me a long, soft kiss. A chill ran through my body. I felt warm, safe and relaxed. He kissed me again. And again. I looked into his eyes as our lips parted. I didn't want to take my eyes off him. Time had stopped.

Spike smiled. "We'd better get you back to school. Isn't Darlene picking you up?"

"Yes," I replied. "I guess you're right."

"Wait here," Spike said. "I'll go get Primo and be back in a minute." He walked away. I breathed deeply and leaned back on my hands.

"Hey, Marci! Is that you?" Patrick called up to me from the beach. "I've been looking all over for you. What are you doing up there?" I turned around and looked down at him. "Come on down here." He flashed a smile at me.

"No, thanks," I called back. "I found a ride back to school."

"What do you mean?" He sounded annoyed. "We came together. You can't just leave."

"Sorry, I've got to go," I told him. Spike was wheeling Primo toward me. "Maybe I'll see you at school sometime." I stood up and walked over to Spike. I didn't turn back.

Spike helped me climb onto the front bar. Then he leaned over and kissed me on the cheek.

"Happy Valentine's Day," he said.

And it was.

JAN GELMAN, lugging a laptop computer around the world, wrote *Marci's Secret Book of Dating* while living in the rice fields of Bali, on the beaches of Thailand and amid the history of Jerusalem. Jan has been working as a writer since her freshman year in college. She has been an editor, writer and photographer for various newspapers, and is the author of eight books for young readers, including *Marci's Secret Book of Flirting—Don't Go Out Without It*. She is currently living in New York City and working on the third installment of Marci's adventures.

Is there a trick to finding Mr. Right?

Marci's Secret Book of Flirting (Don't Go Out Without It!)

by Jan Gelman

Now that they're in junior high, Marci and Pam know their dating careers should be starting. What they don't know is how to *get* them started. How will they actually meet boys? They decide to ask Marci's former babysitter, Cathy, for advice, and she comes through with flying colors. Soon Marci and Pam are learning how to flirt—with step-by-step instructions based on Cathy's expert research. The question is, will their new technique work on Peter, the cutest hunk in the seventh grade, and his blue-eyed buddy, Dave?

BULLSEYE BOOKS PUBLISHED BY ALFRED A. KNOPF, INC.

Friendship isn't always easy...

And the Other, Gold

by Susan Wojciechowski

When eighth-grader Patty Dillman catches a football in the face, she never imagines that it will help her catch a boyfriend! But before she knows it, she and Tim—the thrower of the football (and a hunk!)—are quite an item. Patty is thrilled, and devotes her time (which used to be spent getting into trouble with her best friend, Tracy) talking to Tim, thinking about Tim, and daydreaming about Tim. So where does that leave Tracy? Patty won't even talk to Tracy on the phone because Tim might call! Feeling left out and discouraged, Tracy begins to spend time with her friends from the school play—and now Patty starts feeling rejected! Can their friendship survive the greatest challenge known to teenage girls—the boyfriend?

"Refreshing and believable."   —*Publishers Weekly*

"Likable and breezy."   —*School Library Journal*

"Right on target!"   —*Booklist*

BULLSEYE BOOKS PUBLISHED BY ALFRED A. KNOPF, INC.

Patty Dillman's got more boy trouble in...

Patty Dillman of Hot Dog Fame

by Susan Wojciechowski

Patty Dillman is sure she's in love. She's got all the symptoms—every time she sees Tim her hands start to sweat, her heart starts to pound, and her legs turn to Jell-O. But Tim doesn't seem to notice—he's too busy skiing. So, in order to keep her place in his heart, Patty decides to take ski lessons. After all, how hard can it be? But she soon learns that it's going to take more than a few quick lessons to solve her problems. Between the hours she spends volunteering at the local soup kitchen, babysitting to make enough money to go on a romantic ski trip with Tim, taking ski lessons, *and* trying to keep up with her schoolwork, Patty hardly knows whether she's coming or going. But one thing she *does* know is that she hasn't seen Tim for weeks—and if she's not careful, she may end up losing the love of her life!

"A spirited follow-up to the first book...breezy and entertaining." —*Publishers Weekly*

BULLSEYE BOOKS PUBLISHED BY ALFRED A. KNOPF, INC.